Without looking at him, she hurried out and let out a huge breath as behind her the elevator doors closed and moved away.

She'd escaped. All she'd have to do was avoid him. It was a huge hospital.

Please don't let him be in my ward—

"Natalie?"

She turned, cheeks flaming. He stood before her. He must have gotten off at the same floor.

"Henry."

He gave a small, embarrassed laugh and smiled. Boy, did she love his smile. So warm and genuine. Her attraction to him skyrocketed in that moment, because she knew what lay beneath such a clean-cut, Clark Kent exterior. Henry may be a gentleman, kind and considerate, but in the bedroom? He was a master with a body that was edible!

Damn it, this had all just gotten incredibly complicated! She'd thought him a one-night stand. Her first ever and only. Someone she'd never have to see again. Someone she didn't have to explain her scars to. But this was her new start. Her new job. Her first day, for crying out loud! And she'd Sworn. Off. Men.

Dear Reader,

I'd always dreamed of being a mother when I grew up. I imagined it many times. I even had names picked out: Conor for a boy and Danielle for a girl (though when I actually became a mother, I never used those names—not even as middle names!). I always saw this happening perfectly. I'd be married. In love. My husband, perfect father material. And though I was married and in love when it happened (and my husband was great father material), we struggled to keep a pregnancy.

We experienced losses that almost broke us and when I got pregnant with my eldest son, I was terrified of what the pregnancy would bring and whether we would be strong enough to endure another loss. That feeling, that fear, is the most terrifying thing in the world. It never leaves your thoughts for a moment, until that baby is safely in your arms.

So, for Henry and Natalie, the hero and heroine of this story, I wanted to explore that with them through the lens of fiction and give them the most incredibly happy-ever-after.

Because I got that, too.

I hope you enjoy their story.

With love,

Louisa xxx

MIRACLE TWINS FOR THE MIDWIFE

———

LOUISA HEATON

HARLEQUIN
MEDICAL
ROMANCE

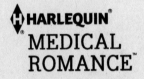

HARLEQUIN®
MEDICAL ROMANCE™

Recycling programs
for this product may
not exist in your area.

ISBN-13: 978-1-335-73760-1

Miracle Twins for the Midwife

Harlequin Enterprises ULC
22 Adelaide St. West, 41st Floor
Toronto, Ontario M5H 4E3, Canada
www.Harlequin.com

Printed in U.S.A.

Louisa Heaton lives on Hayling Island, Hampshire, with her husband, four children and a small zoo. She has worked in various roles in the health industry—most recently, four years as a Community First Responder, answering 999 calls. When not writing, Louisa enjoys other creative pursuits including reading, quilting and patchwork—usually instead of the things she *ought* to be doing!

Books by Louisa Heaton

Harlequin Medical Romance

Reunited at St. Barnabas's Hospital

Twins for the Neurosurgeon

Saving the Single Dad Doc
Their Unexpected Babies
The Prince's Cinderella Doc
Pregnant by the Single Dad Doc
Healed by His Secret Baby
The Icelandic Doc's Baby Surprise
Risking Her Heart on the Trauma Doc
A Baby to Rescue Their Hearts
A GP Worth Staying For
Their Marriage Meant To Be
Their Marriage Worth Fighting For
A Date with Her Best Friend

Visit the Author Profile page at Harlequin.com.

For Nick, my constant support and cheerleader.
Thanks for everything x

Praise for
Louisa Heaton

"Ms. Heaton pens a story that is sure to keep the
reader engaged and cheering her characters on in
their journey to a HEA and this one is up there
with the best.... This really is a beautiful moving
story...I do highly recommend for anyone who
loves a good romance...."

CHAPTER ONE

New York, New Year's Eve

DR HENRY LOCKE would have preferred to stay at home. He liked it there. Home was his refuge. His quiet place. His books were there. His piano. His bed. The apartment was high enough that he wasn't too bothered by traffic noise, but if he was at home whilst rush hour was going on he simply put on some classical music to help drown out the frantic sounds of horns and sirens down on the streets below.

But it was New Year's Eve, and his brother Hugh was over visiting from England, and he'd turned up at Henry's door, insisting that they help to bring in the New Year.

'We're going out! Put on your glad rags, brother dear, we're about to paint the town red, white and blue.'

He'd tried to protest, but Hugh had been having none of it.

'You think I can go out drinking on my own, knowing you're sat at home with your head between the pages of a book? Come on! You're not at the hospital tonight, you've got a rare evening off, so we're going to enjoy it.'

They'd started the evening at an Irish pub called Shamrocks where, to Henry's surprise, Hugh seemed to actually know some of the regulars. It turned out they'd been at university together and so, whilst his brother had knocked back pint after pint, Henry had nursed a glass of wine and smiled and chatted, all the time wishing he was back home in bed, catching up on some much-needed sleep.

Work had been heavy of late. A lot of difficult deliveries, a lot of emergencies. Every time he thought he could finally get some rest in an on-call room his phone would chime and he would get called back to the ward. It didn't help that they were down on staff numbers. Covid had caused a few of the staff to quit. Others had simply migrated to other hospitals.

Ideally, they needed at least one more OBGYN attending, one more registrar, and a couple of certified nurse-midwives. They had agency staff, but that was never the same. All those changing faces, and having to teach new people almost every day, it seemed. HR had just informed them, though, that they'd employed a couple of new people, so that would be good. They needed regulars. They needed people to stay. Then maybe the rest of them could relax a bit more.

That was one of the reasons he hadn't wanted to go out tonight. It was his one night off, his first in God only knew how long, and he didn't want to waste it by spending it doing something he disliked.

And now he was being dragged towards a club that had bass music thumping out so loud he could almost feel his teeth vibrating. It was the sort of thing he hated.

Why, oh, why couldn't Hugh have just suggested a movie instead?

He eyed the exterior of Liquid Nights. A burly doorman stood by the door, checking IDs and occasionally letting people in by unhooking a red rope between two metal poles.

'This looks great!' Hugh said, dragging Henry over to the queue. 'I bet there are lots of lovely ladies inside, just desperate to be blown away by our charming English ways.'

Henry doubted it. Though his own English accent was popular with his patients and his friends, he doubted that Hugh, who was almost struggling to stand upright after his alcohol consumption, would find a lady who might succumb to his drunken charms. But who knew?

It was New Year's Eve and maybe his brother might manage to persuade some lovely local to let him kiss her as the New Year rang in?

Henry checked his phone. Eleven thirty-two p.m. He'd make this his last port of call, then once the New Year was here, convince his brother that it was time for him to go home. He didn't want to be a party-pooper but, as Hugh said, this was his only night off and he'd planned on sleeping.

They slowly made it to the front of the queue and entered the club. Instantly Henry was plunged into a dark, humid and extremely loud room. Hugh turned to him, grinning madly, trying to say something, but Henry didn't catch a word of it. He tried shouting into Hugh's ear that he needed him to repeat it, but it was almost impossible to be heard. Clearly all you could do in this place was drink and dance, as most of the clientele seemed to be doing.

Everyone was up close, bodies writhing and bopping to the music, hands in the air. He smelt sweat and alcohol and the choking smoke of dry ice. As Hugh went in one direction, towards a trio of ladies who appeared to be celebrating a bachelorette evening, Henry headed towards the bar to get himself a drink.

It took some time. There were huge crowds surrounding the bar and his *excuse me* and *sorry* were lost in the noise of the music vibrating from overly large speakers.

Eventually he made it to the bar and waved a note at the barman to catch his attention, successfully managing to order a white wine by pointing at the bottle after the barman had trouble hearing his order.

How did anybody enjoy this?

Looking out over the thick undulating crowds on the dance floor, he thought he spotted Hugh, propping up a wall and trying to charm an amused brunette who was wearing a tiara with pink chicken feathers on it and a pink sash saying *Bride-to-Be*.

Seriously, Hugh? You aren't going to get anywhere chatting up the bride!

He turned back to accept his glass, and was just about to move away and head for a corner as far away from the speakers as he could get when he felt someone stumble over his feet and splash his chest and trousers with a drink from a cocktail glass.

His first reaction was to steady her by catching her arm with his, and then he looked down at his shirt to check the damage.

I should have known better than to wear a white shirt.

A red stain was soaking through across his chest.

Her mouth moved. She said something he couldn't quite catch.

He saw a mass of blonde curls as the woman dipped into her handbag to grab at a handkerchief, and then she began dabbing at his shirt, pressing the material against him here, then there, then lower. Then she paused, bit her lip and looked up at him, and he was suddenly hit by a bolt of *something* as she looked uncertainly into his eyes.

Her lips moved again, forming words he still couldn't hear because of the damned music, and then she nodded downwards. Towards his trousers.

Still shocked by his startling reaction to this woman, he quickly gathered himself and looked down as well. And, yes, there was a small twist of lemon peel stuck to his crotch. He picked it off, and then didn't know what to do with it. Just throw it away?

It was as if his brain wasn't quite working properly, because the woman standing before him was *stunning*. Which couldn't be, because he'd had strong words with himself about reacting to beautiful women just lately, and he'd sworn to himself that getting involved was *strictly* off the menu! There was to be no falling for anyone, no getting romantically attached, no acting on lust, no noticing women, period!

The only women he interacted with were his patients, and his relationship with them was strictly professional anyway.

Henry and romantic entanglements never worked. They always ended badly. He wasn't very good at romance and he struggled with dealing with other people's emotions. So this sort of thing was not meant to happen!

He stood there, kind of dumbstruck, one hand holding his glass of white wine, the other holding the lemon twist. He opened his mouth to speak, to ask if she was all right, but she just shook her head and pointed at her ear. She couldn't hear him either, damn it!

Henry put down his glass, and the lemon twist, on the bar. He wanted to be able to apologise. Wanted to buy her a new drink in case it was his fault that hers had spilt. But this music was far too loud.

He pointed to a door marked *Exit* and she nodded.

He hadn't realised how hot and stifling it had been inside until the welcome cool breeze of outdoors washed over him as they stepped outside. The doorman moved aside to let them pass and they took a few steps to one side of the door.

'I'm sorry about that,' he said. 'You must let me buy you another drink. Or at least pay.'

He began to rummage in his pockets for his wallet, but she reached out and placed a hand on his arm, stopping him.

'No, thanks. I didn't want to be here anyway, so you've helped me escape.'

He smiled. 'You too? I thought I was the only one who didn't want to be here.'

'Clubs not your thing?' she asked, smiling up at him.

She wasn't that much smaller than him. He was just over six feet tall. She seemed to be about five ten. Maybe a little less if you took away the huge amount of blonde curls.

'No, I'm afraid not.'

'Nor mine.'

He nodded in acknowledgement. Glad to be able to talk, rather than shout to be heard. She intrigued him, this woman. He'd never seen her before—but then why would he? His whole life seemed to revolve around the hospital lately, and if you weren't a patient, or a member of staff, then it was sometimes easy to forget that there was a whole wide world out there, full of people and places yet to be met or explored.

'You're... English?' she asked, her head cocked to one side.

'Yes. Oxford born and bred. Henry—Henry Locke.'

He held out his hand and she reached for it.

As he clasped his hand around hers he felt a surge of something undefinable rush through him, so when she let go he placed both hands back inside his trouser pockets, so that he didn't do it again. She made him nervous. She made him consider breaking his promise to himself. He could still feel the imprint of her hand, even though he wasn't touching her any more.

He rocked back and forth on his feet. Kept glancing away, almost as if he were looking for his escape route. And yet...he knew he didn't want to go. Something about her made him want to stay. For just a few moments longer.

'I'm Natalie.'

He smiled. It suited her. 'Pleased to meet you, Natalie.'

'You too. I hope I haven't ruined your shirt.'

'Oh, this old thing? Don't worry about it.'

'You must let me pay for the dry cleaning.'

'Nonsense.'

Behind them there was a blast of noise as the club door opened and out came Hugh with his arm draped around the neck of a hen. He waved at Henry and staggered over.

'Hey, this is Brandy! She and I are going to have a party of our own. You okay to get home, brother dear?'

Henry nodded. 'Fine.'

Hugh blearily peered at Natalie. 'Who's this? Have you pulled?'

Henry looked at Natalie, mortified. 'Please let me apologise for my crass brother. Alcohol appears to have shut down the politeness centre of his brain.'

She laughed—a beautiful sound. 'That's okay. If you can't drink tonight, when can you?'

Hugh and his new lady-friend headed off down the street. Henry felt his cheeks flaming with embarrassment. His little brother always had been the most exuberant member of the family.

'Sorry about that.'

'It's okay.'

They both watched his brother and his temporary companion disappear around a corner.

Natalie shivered.

'Are you cold? Here, let me…' He shrugged off his suit jacket and draped it around her shoulders.

'Thanks.' She snuggled into it.

He felt that he should leave. It didn't matter about the jacket; she could keep it. His brain was screaming at him. *Walk away whilst you can! Save yourself!*

But he found himself staring at her instead. Entranced by her soft blonde curls, and the way shadows contoured her face. The small uptilt to her nose…the soft-looking plumpness to her lips. She wore a dress with thin straps, the colour of midnight and sparkling with sequins, and her feet were in strappy heels. Painted toenails. An ankle bracelet. A small, dainty tattoo on the side of her left foot that he couldn't quite make out.

And then he realised that maybe all the staring was going to creep her out.

'Are you…um…going to make any New Year resolutions?' It was the only question his befuddled brain could conjure up, inoperative as it was in its current confused state.

She nodded. 'Yes. I'm going to start afresh. Not let the past hold me back. I'm going to put everything into my new job and make new friends. Be a good neighbour. Stay away from guys. You?'

'Ah…um…yes. Same. Stay single. Not let my past hold me back, but learn from it…you know, that kind of thing…'

He kept staring into her face. She had the most exquisite eyes and wondered what colour they were. Blue? Green? It was hard to tell at night. But they were bright, and intelligent, and yet also somehow haunted. It was that shadow, that darkness, that intrigued him. It was as if she was trying to mask something—but then perhaps that was the past she'd talked about?

Henry knew all about painful pasts. And the yearning to escape them.

'Ten! Nine! Eight!'

They both heard the countdown begin inside the club.

Henry looked nervously at Natalie. Clearly they were about to ring in the New Year together. Two complete strangers.

'Seven! Six! Five!'

His mind raced. What was the etiquette here? They'd just met, and the standard practice as the New Year was rung in was to cheer and celebrate with those close to you with a hug and a kiss. But they'd both admitted that neither of them wanted to get into anything, so…

If he were to kiss Natalie, how should he do it? On the cheek? On the lips?

He stared at her mouth, torn with indecision.

'Four! Three! Two!'

He looked at her eyes, as if seeking direction. Or maybe just permission. He really wanted to kiss her, despite his rules—because, hey, it was just one kiss, right? It wasn't going to lead to anything. He'd kiss her, wish her a Happy New Year and then leave. He'd be enigmatic. She'd go on with her life and tell her friends about the mysterious stranger she'd once kissed at midnight and he kind of liked that image. Kind of liked being a character in her story, even if it was for the briefest association she'd ever had in her life. It didn't matter that he'd never see her again. Did it?

'One! Happy New Year!'

The roar of voices from inside the club, the cheering and the whistles being blown, caused them both to laugh at how silly it all was. She looked up at him shyly, almost coquettishly, and he knew she wouldn't mind if he gave her a brief kiss.

He smiled and took a tentative step forward, bent his head low and moved in to give her a peck on the cheek. It seemed gentlemanly. Not too forward. Not too brash. Not assuming that she wanted more.

But the skin on her cheek was baby-soft, her hair smelled like flowers, and after he'd pressed his lips to her cheekbone, still with his hands in his pockets, he suddenly lingered, his senses going crazy at her scent, her softness.

She turned to look at him with questions in her eyes. Her face so close to his. She looked down at his mouth, then back up to his eyes again. Uncertain? Hopeful? Wanting?

'I...'

His throat had stopped working. The words couldn't be formed. His breath was gone from his lungs. His senses were all in complete disarray as she reached up to cradle his face and brought his lips back to hers.

He closed his eyes and kissed her.

The sun, already high in the sky, was streaming through his bedroom window when Henry awoke the next morning. He blinked rapidly, trying to clear the sleep from his eyes, his body deliciously content.

And then he remembered.

Turning his head, he saw a mass of blonde curls on the pillow next to him. Natalie was lying on her front, facing away from him, her delicious hair splayed all over his white pillowcase, her bare arms cradling the pillow. The smooth sweep of her back, bare down to the crease of her bottom, where a bedsheet covered her modesty, was marked by a small array of silver scars.

He swallowed hard. As mind-blowing as it had been last night, this was *not* the way he'd hoped to ring in the New Year—by breaking the only vow he'd made for himself!

Not a great start, was it?

Sighing, and rubbing his hand over his face, he turned the other way and picked up his phone to check the time. He couldn't remember setting the alarm. He and Natalie had stumbled into his apartment, frantically removing his shirt and her dress, and they'd practically fallen into bed, unable to tear their hands away from each other long enough to be able to set an alarm.

Nine thirty-four a.m.

He immediately sat up straight, his mind roaring into action. He had a scheduled C-section at midday. Once he'd showered and cycled to work that would leave him cutting it fine, that was for sure.

Henry glanced down at the still-sleeping Natalie. Should he wake her? What would he say? He really didn't want to have that awkward conversation over breakfast, promising to call her when he knew that he wouldn't. If he was going to start this year afresh, he had to forget about this little setback and start anew *today*.

He pushed aside the sheet, grabbed jersey boxer shorts, trousers and a shirt, and headed into the bathroom. He'd wash, shower, brush his teeth… And then apologise for leaving her, explain that he was running late for work, and hopefully avoid the conversation that he just knew she'd want to have.

Would she see him again? Would he call her? They should do this again sometime.

No.

No. No. *No.*

He couldn't afford to do any of that. No matter how amazing last night had been.

Flashes of it coalesced in his brain. Their frantic kisses…her hot breath against his neck. The feel of her as he plunged deep inside and the way she'd arched her back as she gasped…

His body stirred in response, so he turned the shower setting to *Cold* and stepped into the chilly spray, gasping himself and holding his breath as the icy water ran down his body.

What am I doing?

He quickly washed his hair and then stood for a few moments with his head under the spray, trying to gather his thoughts and empty his brain of last night. Okay, so he'd messed up at the first hurdle, but he was a man who believed in second chances, so he had to give himself that opportunity.

Turning off the water, he rubbed his hair with a towel, then dried off his body before getting dressed.

Would she be awake when he went out? Would he have to turn away so she could get dressed? Would he have to have that awful conversation with her whilst his back was turned?

It didn't seem right, but he had to do it. He was a gentleman above all things and she deserved the truth. This couldn't be anything more. They'd had one great night and that was all. It ended here. Memories would have to be enough.

Resting his hand on the door, he took a few moments to breathe deeply, then grasped the handle and stepped out. 'Are you awake? We need to—'

The bed was empty, save for crumpled sheets and askew pillows. He noticed that her midnight-blue sequined dress was gone from the floor and—he padded into the hallway—yes, her high heels were gone, too.

'Natalie?'

There were no signs of her.

She had left. Just like that.

'Maybe she didn't want to have that conversation either,' he mused aloud, not sure whether to be elated or disappointed by her disappearance.

As the elevator took her down to the ground floor Natalie struggled to slip her feet back into her vertiginous heels. The bell pinged, the doors slid open, and an elderly couple came in just as she was pulling the hem of her short dress down to cover more of her thighs.

'Good morning,' she said awkwardly.

The woman raised an eyebrow and said, 'Happy New Year.'

Natalie smiled at them both, aware that the

gentleman—the woman's husband?—was looking at her with a smile on his face.

His wife swiped at his arm with her rolled-up newspaper. '*George!* Eyes front!'

He snapped to it and Natalie stood up straighter, diving into her handbag to grab her phone and check the time.

Nine forty-seven a.m.! Thirteen minutes to get to her first day at work in her new job! What would they say? And she still had to go home to get changed first. She couldn't barrel up to the hospital dressed in this!

She closed her eyes, cringing at her own impulsive and ridiculous behaviour.

Why had she kissed him like that outside the club?

Why? Why did I go home with him? He could have been anyone! An axe murderer!

Though he hadn't looked like one. He'd seemed quite respectable.

But wasn't that what the neighbours always said when they were interviewed on the local news the morning after a newly discovered bloodbath?

He seemed so nice! Kept himself to himself. No trouble at all...

There were messages on her phone. Her mom and dad wishing her well at her new job. One from her best friend Gayle, who still lived back home in Montana.

New Year, new start! I have no doubt you'll be a great success!

How to tell her she'd stumbled at the first hurdle? That she'd headed out for one drink to ring in the New Year and had ended up falling into the arms of a man and *going home with him!*

That wasn't like her at all. Natalie didn't take risks like that. She had sworn off men after Wade's betrayal.

She blamed loneliness. It was a dangerous thing.

She'd moved away from all her family and friends. Leaving them behind in Montana to go and live and work in New York, after securing a post at Heartlands Hospital in Manhattan. Arriving barely a week ago in the Big Apple, she'd moved her few possessions into a tiny stamp-sized apartment and for the first couple of days had been afraid to go out into the streets.

She wasn't used to a bustling big city. She had lived on a farm for most of her life, her surroundings mountains and plains. Back home she could sit with her thoughts in relative peace and quiet. Sit by a stream to think and listen to the birds. There were vast open swathes of ground filled with horses or cattle. Not this metropolis filled with soaring skyscrapers, bumper-to-bumper vehicles, horns blaring, and thousands of people all busy with someplace to go, who thought nothing of bumping into you and passing on by without even an apology.

So she'd stayed in her apartment, eating what little supplies she had brought with her, talking to no one except her family over the phone. She'd missed them terribly. Felt homesickness for the first time after leaving them all the day after Christmas.

But as New Year's Eve had crept closer she'd felt a determination creep into her soul, telling her that hiding away in her apartment was not how she'd imagined her life in the big city. She'd come here determined to go out and claim what she wanted. So, set on ringing in the New Year, her new life and her new job, she'd headed for the first club she could find. Liquid Nights. And she'd made it in, struggled past all those happy people to get to the bar. Ordered her first ever Cosmopolitan, because she'd read about them once. And then, before she'd even taken a sip, she had managed to trip and spill it all over a guy's shirt. A very nice man's shirt.

She'd been *mortified.* Tried to apologise. But their voices couldn't be heard.

As she'd seen his face in the flashes of the light in the club she'd thought, *He has a kind face.* The kindest face she'd seen since moving there. Dark short hair, slightly wavy. Dark-framed glasses. Strong, defined jaw. And he was tall. Over six feet, for sure.

He'd caught her arm as she tripped, steadied her, but he hadn't gripped her hard. His touch had been gentle, steadying, and the second she'd got her footing he'd let go and smiled, despite the Cosmopolitan staining his perfectly white shirt.

He'd made her heart pound. That was for sure! He'd just seemed so…considerate. Gentlemanly. And then he'd tried to say something to her, but the music had been so loud it had been impossible to hear him. He'd been the first person to be kind to her here, and so when he'd indicated they head outside she'd agreed. Even though he was a stranger, she figured she'd be safe if they stayed by the doorman outside. She wouldn't stray from there, she'd told herself. She wasn't stupid.

Outside in the cool air, she'd heard his voice. His accent. British! And had found her first impressions had been correct. He was a gentleman. And he was kind and thoughtful. And he'd listened to her talk. And then the countdown had begun, and he'd kissed her on the cheek, and she'd been so taken by him, so determined to accept who she was now, she'd taken his face in her hands and pressed her lips to his. Just to see. Just to see if kissing him would be as wonderful as she'd imagined it to be!

And it had been. The excitement and the joy and promise of the New Year being rung in had worked a little magic.

It was hard to describe, but if she had to, she would say it had been like two lonely souls finding each other. Finding hope. Delighting in the other. Needing more. Craving more. Neither of them willing to go home to spend the night alone.

Somehow they'd made it back to his place, and even before they'd walked through the door they'd been removing each other's clothes.

Her need for him had been like a raging hunger. As if she'd been starved for too long and somehow believed that she could eat as much as she wanted at this buffet and the calories wouldn't count. Because it was New Year's. It was special. It was a night like no other. And somehow Henry—beautiful, handsome, body-like-a-Greek-god Henry—had understood her needs and her damaged body as no one had ever done before.

She'd believed sex had been great with Wade. Whenever they'd got together their lovemaking had been frantic and wild, and she'd believed it was exciting because they'd taken each other in small snatches of time, in places they ought not to have. A restaurant bathroom. Wade's car. Once they'd even done it outside in the park!

Wade had been her mystery man, from out of town. He'd seemed knowledgeable and worldly and he had made her head spin. She'd not been able to get enough of him, and had wondered if everyone else's relationship was like hers. Full of excitement and raw impulse and spontaneity.

Only now she could see all that for what it was. Wade had never taken her home to his place *because he couldn't.* Their lovemaking had been illicit and thrilling because Wade had been hiding a massive secret. One she hadn't known about.

She'd thought that his obvious desire for her meant that he loved her. That she was special because she aroused so much passion in him! She'd believed wholeheartedly that Wade would ask her to marry him.

Only he couldn't do that either.

But Henry… Henry had taken her back to his place and he had shown her how a man should be with a woman. Their passion for each other had exploded, yes, but he'd also been able to tease her and slow everything down. He'd taken the time to make sure she was satisfied over and over again before taking his own pleasure, and every time she'd thought she was exhausted, and would no longer be able to reach those dizzying heights one more time, Henry had proved her wrong and taken her there, delighting in her every gasp and sigh. They'd laughed together. Giggled. Rested. Then begun all over again. And all her fears that he would see her scars and stop had faded away like magic.

She'd fallen asleep in his arms, sated and happy and strangely feeling completely safe, considering they barely knew one another.

She'd woken with a start to the sound of a door closing, blinking her eyes open and reminding her that she was somewhere strange and not in her own apartment. The events of last night had flooded back and she'd sat up, pulling the white sheets up to cover her naked chest.

Heart pounding, she'd leapt from the bed to look for her clothes. Her dress had been on the bedroom floor. *Where was her underwear?* Grasping the sheet to her, she'd frantically elevated pillows and checked bookshelves, and eventually spotted the black lace undies hanging off the corner of a large medical textbook. The title hadn't registered. Her main thought had been getting dressed and getting out of there before the lovely Henry came out of the bathroom and asked to see her again.

Maybe.

Maybe he wouldn't want to, but either way she hadn't wanted to stay and have that conversation. This was not how she was supposed to have started her new life in the big city. And she'd had no idea of the time! The sun had been up, and she'd been able to hear the traffic down below. She had to start her new job today!

Why didn't Henry have a clock anywhere? And where was her phone?

She'd grabbed her tiny clutch, found her heels in the hallway, where she'd kicked them off, and wrenched the door open. She'd paused briefly in her flight, wondering if she ought to leave a note.

But what would have been the point? Nothing can come of this. I'm staying single, like I promised myself, so I will just have to be a notch on this man's bedpost. A pleasant interlude for two lonely people.

When the elevator doors pinged open on the lobby floor, she raced past the elderly couple and headed outside to get her bearings. She looked left, then right, raised her hand for a taxi and jumped into the back seat of the first one that came along.

'Inwood, please.'

CHAPTER TWO

THE TRAFFIC GODS were kind and the taxi driver got her home in less than five minutes.

'Please stay, I'll be one minute!' she said, then ran inside, unzipping her dress and struggling out of it before her front door had even closed.

She grabbed a pair of jeans, a white tee and a cream-coloured cardigan, and raced back outside to the taxi.

'Heartlands Hospital, please, as quick as you can!'

'Someone dying?' the taxi driver asked with a smirk, looking at her in his rear-view mirror.

'Me, if I don't get there before ten a.m. I'm late for my first day at work.'

'You a nurse or something?' he asked, pulling back out into the road.

'Yes. A nurse-midwife.'

'Guess you'll be seeing a lot of babies in September, then? After last night?'

She nodded, not really listening, as she pulled out her compact mirror to check her hair. Sometimes her curls could go wild and frizzy. Sometimes she'd get awful bedhead. But actually, despite her acrobatics last night, her hair looked decently presentable. She wished she could have had a shower, but she had wet wipes in her purse, so she used those to freshen up her face and remove last night's make-up.

She tried not to think of how Henry might have looked in the shower. She'd heard the water running as she'd crept out. Tried not to let her imagination go wild with images of soaping him down and getting a daytime look at that excruciatingly gorgeous scar-free body of his that had been hidden beneath the plain white shirt and dark pants.

Those muscles...that tight little butt...

By the time the taxi pulled up outside the hospital she felt fresh and ready to go, despite only having had maybe three hours of sleep.

Luckily, her first report this morning would be to HR, not to the ward. She wasn't due to go to the ward until midday. They'd allocated her two hours to get all her paperwork done. Get her ID made. Her picture taken. Sign all the documents she needed to.

God, I'm starving!

She paid the taxi driver and got out, looking

up at the impressive building set in the heart of Manhattan. The façade was all glass and steel, the hospital's name set in dark block lettering just above the entranceway. She was about to go in when the aroma of freshly baked hot doughnuts hit her, and she turned to see a street cart off to one side. She bought a doughnut and began eating it quickly as she headed into the main building, her eyes scanning the list of departments in the lobby. Human Resources was on the third floor.

The doughnut was delicious. Warm, sugary-sweet dough, with powdered sugar and a hint of warm strawberry jelly in the middle. She felt as if she could have eaten three or four of them! But one would have to do as she got into an empty elevator and pressed the button for the third floor.

She brushed her fingers against her jeans to rid them of excess sugar and licked her lips, trying to take in a deep breath and steady her nerves. She'd made it! After all that! The frantic drive home, the frantic race to the hospital… She hadn't screwed up her first day, the way she'd screwed up the start of her New Year, no matter how amazing it had actually been.

She smiled to herself, reliving moments from last night. Almost laughing at how wild and crazy it had been to do something so completely out of character! But it had been worth it. To feel like that. To be carefree and confident in herself again.

She wondered who he was? What he did for a living? Whether he'd been relieved or not to find his apartment empty when he'd emerged from the shower? Was he missing her? Would he have liked to see her again?

Doesn't matter. The answer would have been no. No matter how tempting he was.

She thought about that for a moment and felt sad. She couldn't help it. Despite her vow to stay away from men and not get involved, because she couldn't trust them, she was still an old romantic at heart. And there was a tiny part of her that still hoped that maybe Henry had been the magical prince? The knight to save a damsel in distress?

She shook her head. No. Women saved themselves these days.

But still…he had been amazing.

Ping!

The elevator slowed to a halt to let on some people from the next floor. The second the doors slid open she looked up—and froze, her breath catching in her throat.

There stood Henry. Dressed in a smart shirt and pants, with a body-fitting waistcoat, a *stethoscope* draped around his neck, and a hospital ID clipped to his belt.

For a moment their eyes met, but neither of them could say or do anything! Then, as the elevator doors started to close, Henry stepped forward to grab a door with his hand and stop it, so he could step inside with her. A woman hurried into the lift also, and hit the button for the fourth floor.

Her face flamed with heat. *He was here! He was a medic of some kind...*

Suddenly the image of her panties caught on the corner of a medical textbook flashed into her mind. An obstetrics textbook written by Dr Robert Yang, one of America's leading obstetricians...who worked here at Heartlands...who was one of the reasons she had applied for a job here. With the best. To learn as much as she could.

How had she not realised?

She couldn't look him in the face. She had never imagined she would run into him again. And now she had to stand side by side with him, not able to say a thing, not to explain running out on him this morning.

Ping.

Third floor.

Without looking at him, she hurried out and let out a huge breath as behind her the elevator doors closed and it moved away. She'd escaped! Her explanation could come another time. Or maybe never. All she'd have to do was avoid him. It was a huge hospital.

But, oh, that obstetrics book... What kind of doctor was he?

Please don't let him be on my ward. Please don't let him—

'Natalie?'

She turned, cheeks flaming once again. He stood before her. Must have got off at the same floor as her.

'Henry.'

He gave a small, embarrassed laugh, and then smiled—and *boy, howdy!* Did she love his smile! Warm and genuine. Her attraction to him skyrocketed in that moment, because she knew what lay beneath that clean-cut Clark Kent exterior. Henry might be a gentleman, and kind and considerate, but in the bedroom he was a master. With a body that was...*mmm, edible!*

But she couldn't stand there appreciating that, because—*damn it*—things had all just got incredibly complicated.

She'd thought him a one-night stand. Her first ever and only one-night stand. Someone she'd never have to see again. Someone she wouldn't have to explain her scars to. And it had been better than it had ever ought to be for a first time.

But this was her new start. Her new job. Her first day, for crying out loud! And… She. Had. Sworn. Off. Men. They didn't choose *her*. They didn't put her first. They used her. Thought she was only good enough for a bit of cheap fun, if Wade's actions were anything to go by.

He'd broken her heart. She had been too gullible, too keen to look past the red flags she'd noticed. She had believed him to be the most wonderful person she'd ever met. And now she was doing the same thing with Henry.

Because of one hot night? Because of a charming smile and a scorching body? His ability to give her multiple orgasms?

No. She refused to get lured in again! She'd made a serious mistake with Wade. She would not repeat her past errors.

'What are you doing here?' he asked.

Her mind whizzed with possible lies, but she knew she wasn't a liar—and besides, she knew what it felt like to be lied to. Honesty was the best policy in this situation.

'It's my first day here.'

He nodded. 'That new job you mentioned… Here? Which department?'

He suddenly looked uncomfortable, and she realised that maybe he didn't want her here.

'OBGYN. I'm a certified nurse-midwife.'

'Ah, I see.'

And there it was. He *didn't* want her here! She saw his eyes darken. Saw the way he looked everywhere but at her, as if he were embarrassed or appalled at this news. And, even though she'd expected it, it *still hurt.*

'Look, I know this isn't ideal. For either of us. But it is what it is and we're both grownups; we can deal with it in what I hope will be an adult way.'

She babbled fast, checking all the time to make sure that no one passing by might be listening in.

'We were together one night, had some fun, but that's all it needs to be. We can sweep it to one side and forget about it. We can both get on with our jobs and forget the fact that we've… seen each other naked and done things to each other that maybe, in the light of day, feel a little embarrassing, but…um…the thing is…the thing *is* that we are mature people and we can forget about it and move on. Right?'

As she spoke, she could see he was peering at her. Oddly, at first, and then smiling, as if amused by her words. She wasn't sure what to make of the sudden change, and then he suddenly tapped at his chin.

'Um…you have a little something…' he said.

She frowned. 'What?' She touched her own chin with her fingers and felt, then, the blob of red jelly that she must have missed when eating the doughnut. Her cheeks flamed once again. 'Oh. Thanks.'

She licked her finger clean and wished her heart would slow down a little. Shame was overwhelming her. She did not know how to deal with this. She'd never done it before. Never had to have this excruciating—

'You're right.'

She looked up at him. 'I am?'

'Yes. We need to work together, and to do that we must put last night behind us. As wonderful as it was...' he added quietly, almost sounding wistful.

So he'd thought it was wonderful too? That was good. That made her feel better. 'Okay. Well, I need to get to HR. They're expecting me. And you, no doubt, have a lot to do, too.'

'Prepping for a C-section at midday. Maybe you can join me in the OR, if you have the time?'

She would love to be in his OR! But she didn't want to seem too keen. Or make him think that she was keen on *him*.

'I might still be in orientation.'

'Okay. Well, I'll see you around, Natalie.' He smiled and turned away, heading for the stairs.

She couldn't help but look at his neat little butt as he did so, knowing not only how it looked in the flesh, but also what it was like to touch. And what it was like to bite…

'See you around, Henry,' she muttered, almost in disbelief that this was happening to her.

She'd become a different person with him last night. Bold. Sexual. Revelling in the joy of her body for the first time since the accident. Telling him what she wanted him to do to her. Urging him on and returning the favour in kind, time and time again. Finding the confidence from knowing it was a one-time thing and she'd never have to see him again.

And now they had to be professional and work together.

As if it had never happened.

So, this wasn't ideal. Natalie. A nurse-midwife in his own department. Of all the hospitals, in all the world, she had to be working in his.

It was a complication he didn't need. But they'd both been clear with each other from the very beginning. Neither of them wanted a relationship.

And yet…it was going to be difficult, with his memories from last night still fresh, replaying in full technicolor and high definition in his mind's eye. He could still smell her scent.

Her hair. Her body. Could remember what she tasted like…

And those scars…what has she been through?

He took his time scrubbing for the C-section, turning his thoughts away from the delectable Natalie and reminding himself of his patient and her history.

First time mother with gestational diabetes. Thirty-six weeks. The baby was already estimated at being over ten pounds, so they'd opted for a C-section, as Mum was quite a small lady, only five foot five, and a normal vaginal delivery would be a risk for both of them.

As he headed into the theatre, he quickly scanned the faces, looking for Natalie. She had blue eyes. Would struggle to contain her mop of curls beneath a scrub cap. He knew that now, but he didn't see her there.

He went over to his patient, who already had her spinal block placed. 'How are you doing, Helen?'

'I'm nervous!'

He saw her teeth were chattering, which could sometimes be a side effect of the nerve block.

'That's to be expected, but you're in good hands, and when your husband is ready he'll be here to sit by your side. We won't start without him.'

He smiled at her, knowing how scared she must be. A Caesarean was quite routine for him. He performed many of them each week. But for the patient it was often their first time. Surgery was a big deal, and this operation was considered major abdominal surgery. So many people thought it was something easy, but it could still take its toll on the body and needed a proper recovery time.

He knew, though, that Helen had a good support network at home. Her husband Cole was keen to get stuck in, and both their parents lived close by. Plus, Helen had three older sisters with children of their own, who were all excitedly waiting for her to bring the new baby home and ready to help out.

The door to Theatre opened and in walked the husband, who sat down on the small stool positioned by his wife's head and took hold of one of her hands.

'Ready?'

She nodded, teeth still chattering.

Cole looked up at Henry in question.

'That's normal. So, are we ready to meet your son?'

'Yes.'

'Good.' He took hold of some pincers and pinched at Helen's abdomen, high and low. 'Feel that?'

'N-no. N-nothing.'

'Just as we like it. Okay.' He eyed the people in his team. 'Let's make a start. Scalpel?'

Tess, his scrub nurse, passed him the blade and he made the first horizontal incision. It didn't take him long to get through the various layers. Skin, fat, rectus sheath, the rectus, the parietal peritoneum and then the loose peritoneum, exposing the distended uterus. He opened up the uterus and Tess began suctioning amniotic fluids as he reached in to grab the baby and pull him out. His head was down low.

'You might feel some pressure, Helen.'

'That's okay. I'm doing all right.'

'So am I.'

The head was out. Tess handed him the bulb for suctioning the baby's nose and mouth without having to be asked for it. They were a well-versed team in Theatre, Thankfully, there were no signs of meconium, so the baby wasn't in distress.

When that was done he delivered the baby's shoulders, and then pulled out the rest of him. A very large, chunky baby, wet and slippery, who immediately began to cry. He clamped the cord, cut it, and then held the baby over the blue cloth sheet to show Helen and Cole their son.

'Here he is. Handsome fella.'

'Oh, my God!'

He heard Helen begin to cry and passed the baby to another nurse, who draped him and took him over to the warmer to be fully suctioned, dried, and have some initial tests undertaken, like blood sugar, weight and measurements.

Whilst the others took care of the baby, he delivered the placenta and then began the suturing process, which was probably the longest part of the procedure. Best of all the baby was crying, so were Mum and Dad, and there'd been no haemorrhage. It had been straightforward—just as Henry liked them to be. He would never get bored with C-sections.

When he was done, he spoke to his patient. 'We'll keep you monitored in post-op for an hour or so—just to keep an eye on your vitals and any bleeding, okay?'

She nodded, smiling with happiness.

He went over to the warmer, where Dad was already busy taking pictures with his cell phone. The nurses there were not concerned. All had gone well, and he felt that rush of adrenaline at yet another excellent outcome.

He never allowed himself to get nervous before surgery. His patients deserved him to be on top form. His nerves always came later—afterwards. When the last stitch was in and he could do no more. That was when the enormity of the situation would fall upon him and he would know that he had evaded disaster yet again.

It made him feel good to keep on bringing new life into this world. It was a snub to the darkness that had taken so much from him. A two-fingered salute to what he had faced, losing his own daughter before she had even been allowed the chance to take her first breath.

I've beaten you again.

He scrubbed clean and headed down to his office to write up the notes. He met his mentor Dr Robert Yang on the way, who was dressed in flowing blue scrubs as he himself headed into Theatre.

'All good, Henry?'

'Absolutely. Straight in, straight out. One healthy boy—once we get his blood sugars sorted.'

'Marvellous. That's what I like to hear.'

'You got something good?'

'Patient with uterine didelphys being transferred in from Brooklyn.'

Two uteruses? That was amazing! 'I'd like to see that.'

'I need you to cover the floor as Serena's not in yet.' Serena was another attending. 'But join me when she gets here.'

Robert walked on by and Henry gave a low whistle. Two uteruses! Was the patient pregnant in both? Dr Yang hadn't said. But it would be a historic case to see and be involved in. The kind of thing that made careers. That got your name noticed. And Henry had ambitions. To be the best. To become as well-known and as well respected as his mentor.

In his own office, he sat down and logged into his computer. He began typing, and was lost in his own little world when a voice began to make its way into his senses. He stopped and looked up.

Natalie.

She was being shown around the floor by Roxy, one of the other midwives. 'This is the dirty laundry room. This is Dr Yang's office. And this…'

Roxy smiled in his doorway. 'This is Dr Locke, one of our attendings.'

Natalie smiled at him and came in, hand outstretched as if she'd never met him before. 'Nice to meet you, Dr Locke. I'm Natalie, the new nurse-midwife.'

He smiled at her impressive improvisation skills and stood to take her hand, happy to play along with the pretence of them being strangers. 'Pleased to meet you, Natalie,' he said, trying not to pay too much attention to how it felt to be touching her again.

It was as if there were sparks in the air between them. Electricity tingled through every nerve-ending in his hand, sending bolts of excitement up his arm and straight down to his groin. Clearly his body remembered!

He sat down before it became obvious how excited he was to see her again. He was just in scrubs, after all.

'How did your C-section go, Dr Locke?' asked Roxy.

'Very well. Mother and son doing fine,' he answered, looking directly at Natalie, unable to tear his gaze away.

She'd been a stunner at night-time, but in the daytime she looked amazing! Those unruly curls, her large blue eyes, her face devoid of make-up…she could easily be a model. But she was more than her looks—he knew that. She was kind, and she had listened to him talk, and her laughter when he'd whispered naughty things into her ear had been hypnotic and delightful. It had made him feel as if he always wanted to make her laugh and smile.

Only he couldn't. He *wouldn't*.

Natalie had been his for one night only, and he was not going to allow himself to be drawn into another relationship. He'd rushed into a relationship before and it had ended terribly, crushing his heart and his spirit. He'd taken some time off work to think about what he wanted to do with his life afterwards, and he'd realised his work was what was important to him if he was going to feel any balance at all.

'You're busy,' said Roxy. 'We'll leave you to it. Come on, Nat. Let me show you where the staff room is. There might be some chocolates lying around.'

He watched them go and let out a pent-up breath.

Things had to get easier, surely?

'Dr Locke's delicious, right?' whispered Roxy conspiratorially.

'I guess…' Natalie didn't know how else to respond. Say yes and admit she found him attractive? Or say no and have Roxy think she was weird for not noticing how dishy the attending was? So she'd opted for a safe middle ground.

'He's got that sexy specs thing going on, and you'd think he was this geek, right? But you can tell from his clothes, and when he's in scrubs, that he's got a delicious bod!' Roxy leaned in even more. 'Once, Saffron saw him taking off his scrub top in the changing room and she said he was all muscle with a washboard stomach. I mean…can you imagine?' Roxy feigned swooning.

Natalie laughed and swallowed hard. Saffron

was right. He was exactly like that. And more. But he wasn't just a hot body to be admired. There was more to Henry than that. He'd been kind, funny, polite. A good listener. An attentive lover. Considerate. Neat. And she had no doubt there was a whole lot more to learn about him. Even if she would never get that chance.

I don't want to know more about him. It was one night. That's all.

And, though her experience with her ex, Wade, made her yearn to want to know more, she knew it would be dangerous to do so. What if she thought he was perfect?

Then I'd most definitely be wrong.

'Tell me about Dr Yang,' she said, trying to redirect the conversation.

Roxy chattered on about their fearless leader and head of OBGYN, whilst she made them both a drink in the staff room. Natalie was pretty much ready to start work now. She'd had her orientation, signed all her paperwork, got her ID. All that was left was to start taking care of patients. It would be the best way for her to settle into a new job.

Back home, when she'd first qualified, she'd had to shadow another midwife for a couple of weeks before she could look after her own patients, and it had been only after that point that she'd felt like she had truly started. She assumed the same would be true here. She was keen to get stuck in. She'd come all the way from Montana to New York to start afresh and she just wanted to get started.

This was her new slate. Her new life. Free of all the trauma that Wade had wrought upon her heart and soul. She wanted to be successful here, to prove to herself, and to him, that she was better than all that sordid business he had dragged her into. Ruining her name and her character.

Just thinking about it now made her angry. She'd been the innocent party! She'd believed he'd loved her! How was she to have known his secret? That he had a wife and children in the next town over? She'd thought he loved her. The heat between them had been *undeniable*. A heat that she had mistakenly believed to be love…

But she'd been a naïve fool, and hated herself for not having seen the signs that now, with hindsight, had been all too clear. His only calling her from a cell phone number. Never going to his place. Saying he worked most weekends. No public displays of affection. No shopping and eating in the next town over, and never at any popular places. She'd felt special, and he'd made her feel that way after having lived most of her life back home being ignored or expected not to make a fuss.

That was what happened when you were the youngest of six kids. By the time Natalie had come along, she'd simply had to fit in with the others. No special treatment for being the baby of the family. She'd just been another mouth to feed. She'd vowed to herself that when she grew up and had a family of her own she'd only have a couple of kids. Maybe three, at the most. So that she could give each of them the attention and love that they deserved.

And be the best mother ever.

Wade had taken that from her, too. She'd thought they would settle down and start a family. She'd often dreamed of carrying his child, even though he'd told her that they needed to wait a little longer. That they'd do it one day soon. And worst of all? She'd *believed* him. Fooling herself that they were both heading in the same direction. That they both wanted the same things. To discover the truth had devastated her.

She consoled herself with a chocolate from the tin, and then accepted the mug of coffee that Roxy served her.

'So, what made you come to Heartlands?'

'Well, I live in a very small town back in Montana. We have a medical centre there that

I worked at, but it's a very small department and any patient that was complicated or considered high risk was sent to a bigger hospital, as we didn't have the facilities. That was good for the patients, of course, but it often left me feeling like I wished I could experience more. I enjoy learning new things, and so I started looking to see who else was hiring. I'd never been to New York, so I applied and got the job.'

'That's fantastic. But you'd never been to New York? Ever?'

Natalie shook her head. 'Nor have I ever left the country.'

'You're serious?' Roxy looked shocked.

Natalie laughed and nodded.

'Wow. I mean, I can't imagine not having travelled to other places. Are you, like, a homebody?'

She shrugged. 'I do like being at home.'

She thought of her bedroom back home. The pale pink wallpaper that had been there since her teens. The framed certificates on the walls. The family dog, Scoobs. The horses. Mucking out. Mom yelling at Dad for bringing bits of farm equipment into the kitchen and leaving grease stains everywhere. Dad's heavy sighs and winks at Natalie when her mother wasn't looking. Her sisters borrowing her things. Her brothers hogging the family bathroom every time they went on a date and emerging from it in a cloud of body spray.

It was noisy and raucous at home, but she missed them all anyway.

She'd never, ever thought to leave. Not until Wade had stained her name and her reputation.

'Excuse me…?'

Natalie started at the sound of Henry's voice from the doorway and turned to look at him, her cheeks flushing. Exactly which part of her conversation with Roxy had he overheard?

'I've just been notified of a case of foetal hydrothorax coming up from the first floor. It needs a thoraco-amniotic shunt. Would you like to scrub in, Nurse Webber?'

Natalie looked over at Roxy. 'Would that be all right?'

'Absolutely! Go for it. Learn from the best.'

Nat turned back to Henry. Smiling. 'Yes, please.'

'All right. See you in the OR.'

When he disappeared, it was as if he'd taken all the air from the room. Natalie suddenly felt herself deflate, aware of the way she'd shot to attention when she'd heard his voice. 'Wow. I've never seen that procedure.'

'Nor have you seen his magic hands at work.

I tell you, one glance at him over that surgical mask and you'll fall in love. It's the eyes. And his hands. It's like watching a master at work. We've *all* fallen for Dr Locke. You'll have your turn now.'

Natalie laughed nervously. 'I don't think so.'

'Think you're immune? Think again. Just remember you're safe, though. He doesn't really date. Keeps himself to himself. We reckon there's some big tragedy in his past that he doesn't speak about. Makes him more enigmatic, if you ask me.' Roxy sniffed and glanced at her nails before abruptly changing the subject. 'Want me to show you where the scrub room is, or can you remember?'

'I remember.'

But Roxy's warnings sounded ominous, and now she was beginning to doubt her acceptance to join Henry in the OR.

'Then go get 'em, girl!'

He'd not meant to listen in. But after the call from Dr Fox on the first floor, about a twenty-eight-weeker with persistent fluid build-up in its chest, impacting lung development, he'd called to prep a theatre for the procedure and had heard her voice as he'd neared the staff room.

He'd intended to walk straight past, assemble his team and check to see if Serena was in yet, but he'd heard Natalie talking about wanting to see more complicated cases and before he'd known what he was doing, he'd asked her to join him.

It's fine. I do know what I'm doing. It's just one colleague asking another colleague if they'd like to see an interesting case, that's all.

He was scrubbing his hands when the door to the scrub room opened and she came in, tucking her curls beneath a scrub cap.

She looked up at him hesitantly. 'Hi.'

'Hello.' He reached for the nail pick. Decided to make this businesslike from the offset. 'Patient is a thirty-six-year-old woman, twenty-eight weeks and two days pregnant. Fluid was noticed at the twenty-one-week scan, but it was only a small amount so they decided to monitor and refer to a maternal-foetal medicine doctor, who performed an echocardiogram on the baby. Thankfully there was no mediastinal shift on the heart, but the fluid has built up significantly in the space between the lungs and the chest wall.'

'Okay.' She began to scrub.

'Dr Fox performed a foetal thoracentesis to drain the fluid, but it just returned, so we need to do this procedure now, before there's damage to the lungs and heart.'

'Did Dr Fox take a sample of amniotic fluid to see what might have caused this?'

He was impressed that she knew about that. Especially if she wasn't used to seeing complicated cases. 'He did, but won't get the results back until later today.'

'And what exactly will we be doing?'

'Placing a pigtail catheter into the baby's chest. This will allow the fluid to drain into the amniotic cavity. It gives the best chance of stopping the lungs from under-developing.'

'Okay. How many of these have you done before?'

'About ten.'

'And are they always successful?'

'They have been so far.'

He smiled and then, fully scrubbed and sterile, headed into the theatre to take a look at the scan images that Dr Fox had sent up. It was as if he could breathe again. His heart had been thudding. He could see quite clearly the build-up of fluid in the baby's chest.

Tess helped him gown and glove up, he checked that the mother had received sedation, and then he used the scanner to check the baby's position in the womb, just as Natalie came in, too.

'Come and stand near Tess. Then you'll be able to see everything. Everybody… This is

Certified Nurse-Midwife Natalie Webber, joining us on a permanent basis.'

Everybody said hello. There were smiles and nods.

'Okay, let's make a start.'

He made a small incision in the mum's abdomen through which to pass the needle that contained the catheter. Using ultrasound, he guided it into the womb and into the baby's chest, stopping in the pleural gap where the fluid build-up was. The mother's sedation passed through the placenta to the baby, so the little one was also sedated, and thankfully didn't move during such a delicate procedure.

He looked up briefly at Natalie and saw that she was utterly engrossed in what he was doing. It made him smile. He was all about education. He wasn't grandstanding. But he really wanted this procedure to go well. After all, it was the first time she was seeing him at work, and for some strange reason, he wanted to impress her.

'Deploying the catheter now.'

He pulled back allowing the first part of the catheter to unfurl in the pleural gap, then withdrew a bit more until he was outside the chest wall and in the amniotic space. He deployed the rest of the catheter. It sprang into a recognisable pigtail curl that would help to hold it in place until the baby was born.

'That's amazing,' Natalie said. 'And that will help drain the extra fluid into the amniotic sac?'

He nodded, removing the rest of the needle and stitching up the small incision he'd made in the mother's abdomen. 'We'll keep her under obs for twenty-four hours, then she can go home. In about a week, she'll get a scan to measure how much fluid has been removed.'

He stepped away from the patient, removing gown and gloves. Natalie did the same, depositing hers in the same bin as him before they went back to the scrub room.

'Such a simple thing, yet it works! And the mom didn't even need major surgery for it to happen.'

'Yep. It's done on an outpatient basis.'

'That's remarkable!' Natalie shook her head, as if she couldn't quite believe it.

'Medicine is capable of many remarkable things.'

'It is. But it needs remarkable people to carry it out.'

Her cheeks flushed. He liked that. Was thankful for her compliment. He smiled a thank-you, knowing he had to get out of there before he said something stupid back, like, *Hey, do you want to get a drink later?*

'Well, I must be off. Dr Yang has a unique case that I want to catch up on.'

She nodded. 'Okay. Thanks again.'

'You're very welcome.'

He stared at her a moment more, realising that the more time he spent in her company, the more he liked her, and that it hadn't been an error of judgement when he'd taken her back to his place. There *had* been something special about her. He'd not imagined it.

Natalie was a good person. And potentially a real threat to his vow to remain steadfastly single and not get into any complicated relationships. What had he heard her say? That she came from Montana? A small town? Was here to start a new life in the big city? He didn't want to ruin that for her. She deserved her new start.

'Okay. I'll see you around.'

'You will.'

And he left, heading to his office to write his notes and then track down Dr Yang and the double uterus, determined to think about his work and not the curly-haired blonde who seemed to be at the forefront of his mind.

Natalie had been given the care of a forty-weeker called Felicity. She had been contracting regularly for the last six hours and was here alone, without a birth partner. The baby's trace looked good. It was handling the contractions well. No decelerations or anything to give any concern, and at the last check mom had been eight centimetres dilated.

Felicity puffed on the nitrous oxide as another contraction died down.

'How are you doing, Felicity?'

'Oh, my God, these are killing me!' she said, her head dropping back against her pillow.

Natalie wiped her brow with a cold, damp facecloth. 'Want anything stronger?'

Felicity shook her head. 'No. I can do this,'

'Okay.'

Natalie was just readjusting one of the transducers when Felicity's water broke in a gush.

'You nearly got me!' she said, and smiled. 'But that's a good sign. Things are moving on and some of the pressure should feel better now.'

Felicity began to puff on the nitrous oxide again, as Natalie checked the patient's notes one more time. She liked to be careful. Didn't want to miss anything. Especially on her first patient in her brand-new job!

It was always a worry…that something would go wrong. And working on patients who were placing their lives and those of their children in her hands was always stressful.

People could be litigious in today's society. They complained over the smallest thing. But Natalie had always taken anything like that as a learning opportunity. At her last hospital, back in Montana, a new mother had made a complaint about one of Natalie's colleagues, saying she'd been mean to her during labour. Ordering her about and therefore ruining that mother's birthing experience.

Since that day, Natalie had worked hard to make sure that all her comments and all her behaviour towards her patients were kind and considerate. Because it was a special experience. It was their child's birthday. No matter what, it would be a day that would be long remembered by those parents, and Natalie would have a starring role. She wanted everyone to remember her fondly.

She noted that there didn't seem to be much mention of the father of the baby in Felicity's notes, and clearly he wasn't here, either. Was he just squeamish and waiting at home to celebrate with a cigar? Or was he not in the picture at all?

'I feel like I want to push...' Felicity breathed after the contraction had died down.

Natalie noticed that she was trembling, which could be a sign of transition. She would need to examine her to check that her cervix was fully dilated.

'Okay, let me check you first, though. We don't want you pushing too early, because if there's any cervix left over and you push too soon it could swell up.'

Natalie admired Felicity's strength. Here she was, birthing her baby without a partner. Trying to do it without an epidural or pethidine. Just the nitrous oxide She had spirit and determination.

'You're doing brilliantly, you know.'

'I'm not, though.' Felicity began to tear up. 'Look at me! Here alone! No family. No boyfriend. What kind of mother am I that I'm bringing this child into the world without support? He'll be all alone. No father to teach him things.'

'Hey, now. There are a lot of kick-ass mothers out there bringing up their children single-handedly, without families or partners, and they're doing a brilliant job.'

'I wanted so much more, though. I thought everything was perfect! That I'd get the dream, you know?'

Natalie laid her hand on Felicity's. 'You can make the dream by yourself. Be the best mother ever. If he has you, then this little boy has all that he needs.'

Felicity began breathing in the nitrous oxide again as Natalie checked her.

'You're ten centimetres. You can begin pushing with your next contractions and I'll alert your doctor. It's Serena Chatwin, isn't it?'

Felicity nodded, still breathing in and out on the mouthpiece. 'I didn't have a father growing up,' she wailed. 'I really wanted my son to have one.'

'Can I ask what happened to your partner?' Natalie asked gently.

'He made me feel like a queen. Then I found out he had two other girlfriends, both of whom had also had his kids.'

Felicity looked down and away, as if she was too ashamed to make eye contact. Natalie stared at her. She knew exactly how that felt. That sense of betrayal. That feeling that you'd been such a fool.

'What kind of role model did I choose for a father, huh? It's laughable.'

'He made you feel special. And you believed him. There's nothing wrong in trying to believe in love.'

'But I should have known!'

'How? People who deceive can often be so charming. And we often take others at face value. We want to believe the best of them. No one goes out there deliberately assuming everyone is a liar. Don't beat yourself up about it. You did nothing wrong.'

Natalie picked up the room's phone and notified the desk that Dr Chatwin's patient was about to start pushing.

'She's in a C-section. We'll send in Dr Locke. He's free.'

Natalie's heart pounded against her chest at the news. 'Okay. Thanks Roxy.'

She put down the receiver and watched the CTG tracing as Felicity's next contraction built, tracing the shape of a very jagged, very high mountain on the paper.

'You need to start pushing with the next one.'

'I'm scared.'

'Don't be. I'm here with you, and Dr Locke will soon be here to help, too.'

The contraction ebbed away. 'What about Dr Chatwin?'

'She's in surgery. But Dr Locke is very good, I promise you. He's very kind.'

'Okay...'

'So, when the next contraction comes along I need you to take in a deep breath and push down into your bottom. And you're going to try and do that three times with each contraction, okay? I'll help you.'

Felicity nodded.

The next contraction began to build.

'Okay. Deep breath in and…push!'

Felicity bore down and Natalie began to count to ten, watching and checking at the same time to see how well her patient was pushing. Sometimes first-time mothers didn't always push in exactly the right place, but Felicity seemed to be doing very well. The baby's head was already there and she could feel hair.

Behind her, there was a knock at the door.

'Come in!' she called.

The door opened and there was a small swish of the curtain as Henry came into the delivery room. 'Hello, Felicity. I'm Dr Locke. Keep doing what you're doing and I'll get ready.'

Natalie felt her body become aware of his presence behind her and she wanted to turn and watch him, to soak him in, as if just looking at him would somehow allow her to feel full and sated. But she couldn't. Her patient came first. So she concentrated instead on coaching Felicity and counting to ten and soon it actually became quite therapeutic.

'How is she doing?' asked Henry.

'Pushing well. Baby's head is right there.'

Natalie stepped back, so that Henry could sit on his stool at the end of the bed, and moved to the side to hold one of Felicity's legs.

'You're doing brilliantly, Felicity. Baby is right here—want to feel?'

Natalie watched as Felicity reached down to feel her baby's head. 'That's him?' Her face lit up with wonder and awe.

'That's him. He's so close now,' whispered Natalie. 'Here comes another contraction. Breathe in. And now push! One…two…three…'

Natalie couldn't help but remember the countdown that she and Henry had listened to outside Liquid Nights on New Year's Eve. She'd felt so nervous, hearing the numbers drop, knowing that most people would find someone to kiss as the New Year arrived and the only person she could do that with was the man upon whom she'd spilled a drink. A man she didn't know at all. A man who had introduced her to the pleasures of the flesh in a way that Wade never had. Because those pleasures with Henry, as far as she could tell, had been honest.

But he was a man she now had to find a way to work with, without letting what had happened between them complicate matters. And she knew, watching him work now, that that was going to be very difficult indeed.

She helped mop Felicity's brow as Henry took over coaching her through her contractions. She noted the laser-like intensity in Henry's eyes as he focused on his work. Trying to ensure that Felicity didn't tear as she began to crown.

'That's it. Little bit more. Little bit more. Tiny push…and pant!' He nodded, the skin at the corners of his eyes creasing as he smiled. 'Head's out. One or two more pushes and your son will be here.'

Felicity nodded, her determination now on show, knowing that the finishing line to all this pain, all this discomfort, was nearly in sight, and that the grand prize—her very own baby— was within reach.

'You're amazing,' encouraged Natalie, dabbing at Felicity's face and offering her a sip of water through a straw. 'You're about to be a mom,' she whispered, smiling and, as she always did since the accident, feeling a pang of envy.

'Another one's coming!' Felicity said.

'Okay… First shoulder's out…can you push again for me?'

She bore down with a groan, and suddenly out came her baby boy, along with a whole lot of hind-waters that splashed all over Henry.

Natalie looked up at the wall clock. 'Three thirty-two p.m.'

Like the gentleman he was, Henry didn't even mention it, or react. He clamped the cord, cut it, and then draped the baby on Felicity's chest. Where her son began to cry, loudly, in protest.

'Oh, my God, he's so tiny! And so beautiful!'

Natalie draped a small towel around the baby quickly, so that he didn't lose too much body heat, smiling as she did so, and rubbing the baby boy's back to help his lungs. She then used a bulb to suction fluids from his mouth and nose, but it was clear the baby wasn't having any problem with his breathing. He was letting everyone know that he wasn't happy about being evicted from his cosy womb.

'Well, his lungs are fine,' Natalie said, still drying him off.

Felicity looked up at her. 'Thank you so much for helping me.'

'Hey, you did all the work.'

'But you got him here safe. You and Dr Locke. Thank you. Thank you so much!'

Henry smiled. 'Has he got a name yet?'

She nodded. 'Wyatt. Wyatt Edward, after my grandfather.'

'That's perfect. It suits him,' Natalie said, smiling.

'Do you want a shot of Syntocinon to help get the placenta out?'

Felicity nodded, and Henry quickly injected it into her thigh. But she hardly seemed to notice, so wrapped up was she in admiring her baby boy. Just as it should be.

'You've got a very minimal tear here, but it should heal on its own. You did great.'

Wyatt was just beginning to settle down, his initial protest now calmed as he lay against his mother's chest and heard her reassuring heart-beat.

'I need to weigh and measure him,' said Natalie. 'I'll just take him for a moment and then you can have him right back, okay?'

Felicity nodded again.

By the time Henry had examined the placenta and checked Felicity's bleeding there was nothing more to do, so he gently covered her with her blankets and offered her another sip of water.

'I bet you're dying for something more,' he said.

'Coffee would be great.'

'I'll see if I can get one rustled up. How about some toast, or a sandwich?'

Felicity smiled gratefully. 'Yes, please—whatever's easiest.'

'I'll go and sort that out for you.'

Natalie watched Henry go, surprised that he was doing that. Usually providing the after-birth nourishment was something that fell to the midwives. At her old hospital the doctors would come in, perform the important part of delivering the baby, and then disappear again.

It was the midwives who did all the duties of tending to their patients afterwards. She liked that about him. It was nice and considerate.

Baby Wyatt was doing well. He had an APGAR of nine, his reflexes were all there and he was a healthy weight. Wrapping him up in a new blanket, she carried him back over to Felicity.

'Here he is. All seven pounds and two ounces of him.'

'Wow. It's hard to think that moments ago he was inside of me.'

'Crazy, isn't it?'

Henry came back with a small tray. There was coffee, a plate with two biscuits on it, and a pre-packaged sandwich. 'Egg salad was all that was left, I'm afraid.'

'It's fine. Thank you.'

'How's your pain level?'

'I'm sore, but I'm fine.'

'Well, if you need anything, use the call button and one of these fine ladies can organise some painkillers for you.'

Natalie smiled at him and then he left.

'Is there anything else I can get for you?' she asked Felicity.

'No. I have everything I need.' Felicity stared down at her son, as if unable to tear her eyes away.

'Okay. I'll give you some time together, and then someone will come round to take you to the postnatal ward.'

'Thanks.'

Natalie gathered her notes and quietly left the room. The birth had gone brilliantly and mother and baby were well, which was the most important thing. She sat at the desk and began to fill in the delivery notes and update the board.

'Hey, how'd it go?' asked Roxy as she passed, carrying an armful of linen.

'Healthy baby boy.'

'Great! Find everything okay? Need any help?'

'I'm good.'

'Fantastic. When you've updated the computer, why don't you go take a break? About twenty minutes?'

'Perfect. Though you might have to point me in the direction of the hospital cafeteria.'

'So, tell me about the blonde,' said Hugh, who had called on Henry's mobile as he sat in the cafeteria.

He decided to play innocent. 'What blonde?'

'The one I saw you with last night! Curly-haired, doe-eyed... Tell me you got yourself a piece of that.'

Henry rolled his eyes. His brother could be

so crass sometimes. 'I wished her a Happy New Year.'

'Yeah, with what body part?' Hugh laughed. 'Seriously, mate, it was good to see you looking that way.'

'What way?'

'Interested in another woman. After what happened with Jenny you deserve some happiness, bro.'

'Thank you.'

'I mean it. What happened was awful. No denying it. Losing the baby…everything. But it's been killing me to see you alone all the time when you've got so much to give. I was happy for you.'

Henry smiled sadly. 'At times I thought I'd never get through it.'

'But you did—and look at you now. In New York. In your dream job. Seeing in the New Year with a hot blonde. So, tell me, was she good?'

'A gentleman never tells.'

Hugh laughed. 'Aha! So she was! You dog!'

Henry grinned at his brother's enthusiasm. 'How was your…erm…date?'

'Awesome. I'm in her bathroom as we speak.'

At that moment one of the radiologists stopped by his table. A young woman. Very attractive, clearly wanting to speak to him. 'I've got to go.'

'We'll speak later, yeah?'

'Yes.' Henry clicked off his phone and looked up.

There was a radiologist, judging by her uniform, talking to Henry. Natalie had sought him out in the cafeteria and was now waiting for the young woman to finish flirting with him—which was clearly what she was doing. The young lady was smiling a lot. Laughing. She played with her hair at one point, and kept tucking it behind her ear. And then she even reached out and touched Henry, trailing a single finger down his forearm.

Unbelievable.

She watched Henry curiously, trying to gauge his response. Wondering whether he would respond to this obvious flirtation in kind? Whether he would draw a slip of paper from his pocket and scribble down his number to pass to this woman? Something…

But with Roxy's words echoing in her brain—*he doesn't date*—she saw Henry shake his head, looking back at the woman with apology.

Natalie watched with bated breath to see what the woman would do next. She shrugged, smiled, then walked away—and Natalie let out a huge breath that she hadn't realised she was holding.

After waiting a moment or two, she carried her tray towards him and stood beside him. 'May I join you?'

He looked up, smiled, and indicated that she could sit.

'Thank you.'

'You're welcome. How's your first day going?' he asked, sounding as if he was really interested.

'Well, I had an awkward encounter earlier on, but I think I survived it—despite the blob of jelly on my chin the whole time.' She smiled and sipped at her drink. 'And then I got to see a fabulous surgery, so that was good too, and then I helped deliver a baby. So...excellent.'

He smiled at her, and there was genuine warmth in his eyes.

'How's *your* day going? Do you always get hit on when you're on your break?'

'Oh. You saw that?'

'Everyone did.' She smiled back.

Was he blushing? It was the darnedest thing! Cute, too.

'That was Amelia. We worked on a case to-gether a few days ago. She's nice, but...not my type.'

'And what is your type?'

He looked up at her and raised an eyebrow.

'Curly-haired blondes who spill drinks on you?' she asked.

She couldn't believe she was flirting with him herself, but it was as if she couldn't stop herself. There was something about Henry that just brought it out of her—and hadn't he already seen who she was? Every excruciating inch of her...scars and all?

Henry laughed and pointed at her coffee. 'Just don't spill that on me. That's all I ask.'

'I'll try not to.'

He was looking at her tentatively. As if he had something to ask but wasn't sure about whether he could. But right now she was feeling brave, so...

'Go on. Say what it is you want to say.'

'I noticed your scars.'

Ah. Here we go.

'Yes.'

'What happened?'

'A car accident. I ended up having a lot of surgery.'

'And are you okay now?'

She smiled. 'I'm getting there.'

CHAPTER THREE

'So, TELL ME how it's going. Is everybody nice?'

Natalie lay back on her couch, holding the phone against her ear as she chatted to her mom. 'It's going great. And yeah, Mom, everybody's nice.'

She couldn't help but think of Henry. The shock of discovering he worked there. The embarrassment of standing in front of him with jelly on her chin on that first day. The tactful way he'd told her about it. The way he'd invited her into the OR. Watching him deliver a baby, unable to tear her gaze away. Flirting with him in her breaks. Seeing him in the corridors each day.

It was getting harder and harder to pretend that nothing had happened between them.

'And you've made friends? I've always heard that people aren't that friendly in big cities.'

'I've made friends. There's a great midwife called Roxy. She's funny and kind.'

'And?'

'And what?'

'What about the doctors? Anyone…interesting?'

'Mom.'

'What? I'm just asking if the doctors are nice!' she protested innocently.

'No, you're asking me if there are any nice men here. And, if you don't mind me saying, you're being very stereotypical. A lot of doctors are women.'

'I know, I know!'

There was a brief silence, as there always was when Natalie and her mother tiptoed around each other, so as not to cause offence. It was even more important now, what with them being miles away from each other.

'You know what I'm asking. This is hard for me. Do you know how it feels to have you all those miles away so I can't see if you're doing okay? If you're looking after yourself?'

'You never worried about that when I lived at home.'

'Because I could see you every day with my own eyes. I didn't have to worry.'

'And now you do?'

Her mother sighed, impatiently. 'You're alone in a big city. Of course I worry.'

Natalie didn't know what to say. She'd never

felt noticed by her mom. Had never heard her mother say that she worried about her. But what if she just hadn't seen it from her mother's point of view?

'I'm doing fine, okay? Don't worry about me.'

'Well, I'm going to, anyway. What are your neighbours like?'

'My neighbours are quiet. There's a Russian lady who lives next door—Mrs Petrovsky. She brought me over a welcome bowl of borscht.'

'What's that?'

'Some kind of beetroot soup.'

'Oh. And work's fine?' she repeated.

'Great. Busy. Complicated.'

'You wanted "complicated" from what I remember.'

'I certainly got it,' she said wryly, thinking about Henry, but knowing she couldn't tell her mother about him.

'You went through a lot, honey. What that man did…he changed your entire life. Your whole future! I'm allowed to ask if there's any chance you're going to be happy there.'

'I know.'

She appreciated her mother's concern. Back home, when she'd been recovering from the accident, not too much had been said about what her injuries meant for her future. Her parents had brought her home from the hospital and everyone had nursed her, yes, but no one had actually spoken about what it all meant, only said, *'It'll all work out. You'll see.'*

She'd wanted to rage at them sometimes. How did they know? They couldn't! Their words were empty and nonsense.

Now... It just made her uncomfortable.

'I'm not looking for a relationship, Mom. You know that. I'm just here to work.'

'Well, just try and make good friends, okay? You've got used to pushing people away since the accident, and you don't want to be all alone in the big city.'

Was her mom right? Did she push people away? Maybe she was a little prickly, but wouldn't anyone be? Her whole world had come crashing down. Her whole future had changed because of a man's lie. A man she'd trusted with her whole heart. And he'd ruined it. Ruined everything. And had there ever been an apology from him? No.

'Mom, please don't. I don't want to argue with you.'

She'd woken with a headache this morning and, despite a good seven hours' sleep, she still felt tired. There was a deep ache in her body that didn't seem to disappear, despite all the body stretches and yoga she attempted. So her irritation was at surface level. Her mom didn't need to do much more digging.

'I don't want to argue with you either. It's just…'

'Just what?'

'Let us be here for you, honey. Even if we are miles away, we're still at the end of the telephone. All you've got to do is call.'

Her mother sounded so sincere, so caring and loving in that moment, Natalie could almost have cried. In fact, she could feel the tears building up behind her eyes, the backs of them stinging and watering as she fought to keep them contained. There was a painful lump in her throat.

'Thanks, Mom.'

There was a silence at the other end. Maybe her mother was fighting the same reaction? That made her smile a little. Perhaps she had misread her mother all along? Maybe she hadn't ever ignored her—she'd just been busy? She'd had six kids. Had a house to run, a job of her own. Perhaps her childhood hadn't been as bleak as she'd imagined? She had had a roof over her head and food on the table every day. So what if affection and love hadn't been shown all that much? Perhaps her parents had showed her that they loved her in other ways? Like her mother was right now?

'I've got to get ready. I'm due in for my a shift.'

'Okay. Well, take care, and promise you'll call me at the weekend?'

'I will. And…thanks. For everything.'

'My pleasure, honey. Love you. Bye.' And then her mom was gone.

Natalie put down her phone and stared at it for a moment. Had she been so wrapped up in her own suffering this year that she'd forgotten what her accident had meant to her parents? They'd nearly lost her, after all.

How had they felt, receiving that call from the police and being told that she'd been involved in a terrible accident? They must have felt awful. Terrified. But had they shown it? No. Natalie had woken up in the ICU, covered in wires and tubes, and her mom and dad had been sitting by her bed, smiling, holding her hands and telling her that she was going to be okay. That they were going to get her through this. And they had visited every day. Steadfast. Stoic. Accepting all the news that had been delivered to them.

My God. Why didn't I notice that before?

Because she'd been hurting, that was why. So wrapped up in losing the man she'd loved and then hearing from the doctors that her abdomen and pelvis had been so damaged in the accident that it was extremely unlikely that she would ever fall pregnant.

The physical scars on her body showed some of her pain, but she knew the scars on her heart were just as bad.

She was a romantic. She'd always dreamed of love. Of finding her prince and settling down and having babies with him one day. It might seem old-fashioned to some, but she was an old-fashioned gal.

She'd wanted it all. The white picket fence. The two point four children. A dog. Maybe some backyard chickens. A house with cherry trees in the garden. A husband who loved her, adored her, and would make the most wonderful father, cradling her belly as her pregnancy grew, just as excited as her to see who they had made together.

All of that gone. Taken from her. By Wade. The most deceitful bastard she'd ever had the misfortune to meet.

Her cell beeped, reminding her she had ten minutes to get to work.

She stood in front of her bathroom mirror, running her hands through her curls, and then stared at her pale face before splashing it with cold water to try and freshen up. Her eyes had gone a little red, but hopefully that would have passed by the time she got to work.

* * *

Henry was locking up his bike when he noticed Natalie heading into the hospital. His first instinct was to call out her name and catch up with her, but he managed to stop himself just in time. Instead, he watched her go in alone, and then waited a few minutes to ensure that he didn't have to share a lift with her.

Because the last three weeks had been really difficult!

Difficult in that he'd begun to realise that Natalie was more than just one hot night. She was fun. And popular. Everyone at work spoke about her kindness to her patients—something he'd witnessed himself—as well as how nice she was as a colleague. She'd really fitted into their little obstetrics family so well. She was generous and friendly. Her laughter made everyone smile, and she was a hard worker, too, putting one hundred percent effort into everything she did.

He'd met her in one of the corridors yesterday, coming towards him. He'd seen her before she'd seen him, and just as he'd decided to turn around and go another way she'd looked up through her curls and smiled at him and—*bam!* It had been like being socked in the gut.

All he'd been able to do was smile and say, 'Hi, how are you doing?'

'Good, thanks. Busy, you know?'

'Yes, yes. Me too.'

It had felt so awkward. When he'd wanted it to be anything but. He'd opened his mouth to say something else. *Anything else!* But he hadn't been able to think of what to say, because he'd been so busy fighting his brain, which had wanted him to yell, *I'd love to see you again.*

But there was no way in hell he was going to say that. His mind and his body would just have to get used to that fact—because he didn't date colleagues. He didn't date full-stop. Despite all the flirting in their breaks. Despite the secret smiles they often shared.

'I...er...must get on.'

He'd waved a manila folder at her, as if it were the most important document on the planet, and passed on by, cursing himself for being an idiot and knowing she must think him one, too.

So he didn't need to run into her again, after yesterday's little debacle.

He counted to ten. Slowly put his cycling helmet into his backpack. And then he strode into the hospital, his eyes scanning the lobby area for her and noting, to his relief, that she wasn't there. He pressed the button for the lift and waited.

'Hello, Henry.'

He jumped and turned to see Natalie standing beside him, holding a takeaway cup and straw. She must have gone to the hospital coffee shop before heading up to their floor.

'Hey. Hi. How are you?' He could feel heat filling his face.

'Ready for another shift!'

The lift pinged its arrival and they both stepped inside, along with four other people.

The silence was incredibly uncomfortable for him. His body was so aware of her proximity, his senses going into overdrive at the aroma of her body scent. Something floral. Spring meadowy. That kind of thing. And on her...

Dear God...

He needed to think of something else. *Quick.* So he began listing the bones in the human body. Alphabetically, to make it harder.

Er...calcaneus, capitate bones, carpals...

On the second floor two people got off, giving the rest of them more room, so he sidled over to the back corner of the lift, hoping she wouldn't notice, giving himself some respite from her delicious scent.

An image danced in his head of rushing over to her and kissing her, pressing her up against the back of the lift...

Cervical vertebrae, clavicle...

She moved to take a sip of her drink, gently enveloping her straw with her full, soft lips. He couldn't help but look. Saw thick pink fluid move up the straw. Strawberry milkshake? He looked up at the roof of the lift, trying not to think of her lips and what they had felt like on his body all those weeks ago.

Coccyx, cuboid bone...

Another ping and they were at their floor. He held back, trying to think about how he could avoid having to walk with her into the department.

She turned to look at him. 'You not getting off here?'

He swallowed hard at the easy double meaning. 'Er...no. I've got to go and check on a patient who came in through the ER yesterday.'

'Oh, okay.'

The lift doors slid shut on the sight of her sucking at the straw again and he sagged back, as if all his breath had left him in one go.

What was it about her that kept alerting him? Kept turning his body on? They'd had one night.

It wasn't the first time he'd had a one-night stand. Occasionally he indulged in them—once he'd made it absolutely clear to the woman that it would go no further than that one night. He had fun, he got the urge out of his system, and he moved on. But *Natalie*?

Was it because they worked together and he kept seeing her? She'd just started here, so it wasn't as if she was going to leave, and neither was he—he'd come here to work under his mentor, Dr Yang.

So I need to accept that I'm going to see her every day.

But how? When she kept smiling at him the way she did? When he could barely control his body's craving to have more of her? Even though that went against every rule he had? What did other guys do when they had to keep on seeing a woman they'd slept with in a professional setting?

Henry got off at the next floor, even though he didn't need to be there, and went over to the large glass frontage of the hospital and looked out. Relaxing his shoulders, he let out a long sigh, then gave himself a stern talking-to. Was he really going to try and avoid her every time he saw her? It was hardly the adult thing to do. No. He just had to get on with it—and that meant no more hiding but treating her the way he treated everyone else. As friends.

So he turned around and headed for the stairs, trotting down the flight of steps that would bring him to his own floor. Sucking in a deep breath to reinforce his new attitude, he stepped into the OBGYN wing with renewed vigour.

He had nothing to fear. Natalie didn't want anything from him. It had been just a bit of flirty fun. Their night together was *over*. She was settling into her new job and doing well. He needed to get on with his own.

He consulted with Dr Yang on the patient with a double uterus. He'd been able to perform the ultrasound scan and discovered that she was pregnant in one, but had a smallish fibroid in the other, which shouldn't cause any problems.

Then he sat in an outpatients clinic for most of the afternoon, seeing his list of patients who were considered high risk. Multiples. Gestational Diabetes. A baby with spina bifida.

When he was done and it was almost time to go home, he went to the staff room to make himself a hot drink as he'd not had one all day.

The door to the staff room was open and he noticed Roxy whizz by. 'Hey, what's the rush?' he asked.

She stopped briefly in the doorway. 'We're swamped! I don't think any of us have managed a break all day. I was just going to relieve Penny and hand over to the night shift.' She eyed him by the kettle. 'Don't suppose you'd be willing to make everyone a drink and take it to them in the delivery rooms, would you? I know it's a big ask.'

'It's fine. I don't mind doing that at all. You go and let me take care of it. How many midwives are on?'

'Nine.'

He nodded. 'Do they all drink coffee?'

'Is the Pope Catholic?' She laughed and glanced at her fob watch attached to the front of her uniform. 'Got to go. Can I leave that with you?'

'Absolutely.' He smiled as she whizzed away again.

Sometimes it could get ultra-hectic on OBGYN. Every room would be filled with a labouring mother, and somehow they'd all go into late labour at the same time, so it was imperative that the midwives stayed with their patients.

He didn't mind making them all a drink. In fact, he knew they'd be appreciative of it, and he liked to support his colleagues, whether they were consultants or porters. The position they held in the hospital didn't matter to him. People were people, and he believed in treating everyone the same.

He managed to find nine clean mugs and made nine hot drinks, placing them on a tray with a jug of milk and a small bowl of sugar, as he wasn't sure who had what.

He began his round, knocking on doors and delivering drinks to thankful midwives. Danielle said she could kiss him. Carlita gave him an appreciative hug. Janine called him a godsend. At the fourth room he knocked on the door, and when he heard a voice call, *'Enter!'* knew he had located Natalie.

'Just me,' he said popping his head around the curtain. 'I offered to do refreshments for everyone.'

'Oh, wow! That's amazing. I haven't had a sip of anything since midday, and my stomach thinks my throat has been cut. Thank you so much!'

He laid the tray down next to her. 'I didn't know how you took it, so help yourself to milk and sugar.'

Natalie took a pink mug, emblazoned with a slogan that said *World's Best Midwife* and added a small splash of milk.

He thought she looked a little tired, but if she'd been on the go all afternoon, with no chance of a break, then it wasn't surprising. But even so she still looked beautiful.

She stirred her drink and took a grateful sip, then grimaced. 'Urgh!' She frowned at the mug. 'Is that milk off?' She sniffed at the coffee and turned her face away in disgust.

'Er...no. It was a new carton I opened. Totally in date.'

'Not being funny, but it tastes rank.'

'Oh...' He felt a little embarrassed that his coffee-making skills had not impressed her. 'Want me to get you something else? You need to stay hydrated.'

'Maybe a glass of water?' She placed the mug back on the tray. 'Sorry. I know you were trying to be nice.'

'It's fine. I'll take everyone else their drinks, then come back with water for you.'

'Thank you, Henry.'

She smiled at him and it did things to his insides. So much so that he simply smiled back, grabbed his tray and left the room.

He took a quick sniff of the milk. It was fine. Maybe it was the coffee itself that wasn't to her liking? Maybe too strong, or something?

He delivered the rest of the drinks, then returned to Natalie with a beaker of water, half filled with ice, which brought a huge smile to her face.

'Perfect. Thank you. This is very kind of you.'

'Well, Roxy said you'd all been rushed off

your feet, so...' Henry looked over at the patient. 'Anything interesting?'

'Running like clockwork. She's just taking a nap after having an epidural placed. I'm waiting for someone to take over, then I'll be off home.'

'I think the night shift have arrived, so someone should be along soon.'

'Great.'

She smiled at him again, and he suddenly realised he'd have to think of something else to say to her or make his excuses and leave. And, as he couldn't think of anything to say... 'Well, I'd best be off.'

'Doing anything nice tonight?' she asked.

'Er...no. Well, I'm staying in. Catching up on some reading, maybe.'

'What do you like to read?'

Did she genuinely want to know, or was she just being polite? 'Crime. Thrillers. That kind of thing.'

'Oh, I love those too!'

'I can always recommend a couple of books if you'd like?'

'I would like.'

He smiled back at her—and then she was called over to her patient as she woke from a brief nap.

The woman looked at Henry askance.

'I'm a doctor, but don't mind me. I just came in to see Nurse Webber. I'm leaving.'

'Thank you, Dr Locke. For the drink.'

Her smile went straight to his heart.

He nodded and left the room, telling himself he'd done a half-decent job in not being tongue-tied and genuinely acting like a normal guy who worked with a normal woman.

Surely he'd given no sign that being in her presence still affected him?

Now all I have to do is repeat that each time we meet and it'll be just fine...

By the time she left work that evening Natalie was absolutely shattered. It had been a long eight-hour shift, without a single break. She'd had nothing but the water Henry had so kindly brought to her room, and no toilet break either. Her legs ached, her whole body ached, and she was so hungry she felt sick.

She knew she needed to get something into her system—*quick*. So on the way home she grabbed a pretzel from a street stall and quickly began to gobble it down. Every mouthful of malty dough seemed like heaven at first, but by the fourth bite she began to feel a little strange, and had to stop in the middle of the street and peer at it, to see if it was off, or had gone stale, or something.

The taste it had left in her mouth was odd and, disgusted, she threw it into a trash can and hurried home. Back in her apartment, she rifled through her food cupboard, trying to find something that would appeal. She fancied something sharp-tasting, so crunched her way through a pickle or two, and then decided to make herself a vegetable curry. She had all the ingredients, and even a spare packet of garlic and coriander naan bread, too.

She turned on the radio and sang along to some music as she cooked. The recipe called for one teaspoon of medium curry powder, but she wanted something with a kick, so added two and a half—almost three. She chopped up a red chilli pepper too, and dropped that into the mix, along with extra cumin.

It smelled delicious, and her empty stomach rumbled in anticipation as she served herself a huge bowl of the stuff, with some soft, fluffy jasmine rice, and settled down to watch some trash television.

The food hit the spot perfectly, taking away her earlier nausea, which she put down to simply not getting a break at work. She'd been on her feet all afternoon, so it was only to be expected; it had probably been a drop in blood sugar.

She didn't recall falling asleep in front of

the television until the noise of a siren racing past her window awoke her to the news that she'd got a stiff neck. She scrambled to her bed and settled down instantly, soon waking to her alarm that went off at six. She had an early shift today, and needed to be at the hospital by seven a.m.

Propping herself up on an elbow, she turned off her alarm and swung her legs out of bed—and suddenly got hit by a wave of nausea.

'Whoa…'

She took some deep breaths and steadied herself as she got to her feet and headed to the kitchen to make herself a coffee. She figured it had to be dehydration. She'd hardly drunk anything yesterday, and when she'd come home she'd eaten and then fallen asleep straight away. So she grabbed a glass of water and necked it whilst she waited for her coffee to brew.

Such a crazy day yesterday! She'd gone from one patient in advanced labour to another. Barely sitting down. On her feet all shift. If she hadn't been tending to her patients she'd been answering phone calls, and had even gone down to the ER at one point, to help assess a seventeen-year-old girl who'd come in with a suspected ectopic pregnancy. Thankfully, it hadn't been. She'd not even been pregnant. It had turned out to be an appendicitis.

Then Natalie had gone back to OBGYN and straight into seeing yet another young labouring woman. The one she'd been with when Henry had brought her that drink.

Bless Henry! What a kind thing to do. Not many attendings would have done that for the midwives, and apparently he'd taken every one of them a drink—which was so considerate. He was a good man and she liked him very much.

She poured herself a coffee and went to take a sip. But when the scent of it hit her nose, she recoiled.

'Urgh! What *is* that?'

She swirled the drink around in the cup, staring at it, trying to work out why her coffee smelt so awful. The same thing had happened at work yesterday, when Henry had brought that coffee. But the coffee at home and the coffee at work were from two separate sources, so the only common factor here was her.

Maybe my tastebuds are changing?

She made some toast with strawberry jelly on it, and thankfully that tasted normal and good, so she ate it in full. She filled a reusable cup with iced water and headed off to work— but not before she picked up a couple of the books she'd read recently, intending to show them to Henry to see if he'd like them.

It was great that their working relationship

was going so well after they'd spent the night together. It showed that they were being mature. That they were adults. She was proud of them both.

But it wasn't easy by any means. It was hard to look at Henry and not think about what he'd done to her that night. How his lips had felt against her skin. The caress of his hands. The weight of him on top of her. The feel of him inside her...

She almost purred just thinking about it...

When she got to work she sat down and listened to the handover of patients from the night shift. There were a lot of ladies in Postnatal now, and only a few labouring. Two in early labour, who were going to go back home and wait for more regular contractions, and two who were staying. Natalie was assigned Shruti Kaur, a first-time mother, thirty-nine weeks pregnant and six centimetres dilated.

She knocked on the door and went in to introduce herself. 'Hello, Shruti. My name's Natalie and I'm going to be looking after you for most of today. How are you doing?'

Shruti smiled. 'I'm doing all right. This is my husband, Kamal.'

She smiled at the man seated beside her bed, who looked at Natalie and raised a hand to say hi.

'Pleased to meet you both. I'm going to take a quick look at your notes and acquaint myself with your case, but if you need anything just ask, okay?'

'Thank you.'

Natalie sat down at the small desk in the room and opened up Shruti's folder to begin reading. The pregnancy had been conceived naturally, right before the couple had been due to begin IVF.

'You got pregnant all by yourselves?' she asked, smiling. They must have been so pleased!

'Yes. We were told I couldn't get pregnant without help as I've got scarred fallopian tubes from pelvic inflammatory disease.'

'Wow. How was that diagnosed? Through a laparoscopy?'

'Yes. They tried to remove the adhesions, but said there was substantial scarring as they were close to the ovaries.'

Removal of adhesions was usually more successful if they were closer to the uterus, rather than the ovaries.

'It says here you tried to get pregnant for four years before you decided on IVF?'

'That's right. We'd had our initial visit at the clinic, and we were all ready to start injections. They always do a pregnancy test, just in case, before they start that, and ours was positive.'

Shruti reached out for her husband's hand and smiled.

'Well, that's amazing. I'm so happy for you.'

And she was. Truly.

It could be a real shock to hear that you might not be able to have children. After her own accident, she'd come around in the ICU to be told she'd suffered tremendous damage to her pelvic area. Her pelvis had broken in three places, her uterus had been torn and her fallopian tubes damaged. Surgery had also removed one ovary. The attending had sat on her bed and gently explained that the likelihood of her getting pregnant without help was extremely low.

'It would be a miracle,' he'd explained softly, as tears had run down her cheeks.

'But miracles can happen,' she'd argued.

He'd nodded, yes, but in his eyes she'd seen that he thought she was deluding herself. In that moment, she'd hated him. Hated all her doctors. Hated Wade!

Miracles can happen.

It was something she'd clung to, desperately at times, because more than anything she wanted to be a mother...

A sudden hot sweat bloomed all over her body, and she realised that she needed to eat something quickly or she was probably going to be sick.

'Would you just excuse me for a moment?' she said, forcing a smile before rushing from the room and hurrying into the staff room.

She needed her locker key, but she was all fingers and thumbs and dropped it on the floor before she could get it into the lock. Then the key got stuck, typically, and she had to slam at the locker door with her open palm before it would turn.

There was a cereal bar in there, with dried strawberry, cranberry, and white chocolate chips. Probably not the most healthy of snacks, but it would do.

Bam! The lock opened and she rifled through her bag to find it. She ripped it open and took a large bite, sighing as she chewed, feeling her stomach settle and wondering just what the hell was going on.

The coffee tasting odd...the pretzel...the tiredness...the nausea this morning... It was almost as if—

No. It's not. It can't be.

Pregnant. That was the word that had bloomed in her mind. But that was impossible. Because the doctors had said it would be a miracle. But...

Miracles can happen. That's what I said.

No. It couldn't be that. She thought back to

her night with Henry. They'd used protection. There'd definitely been condoms.

And condoms are...what? Ninety-eight percent effective?

Ninety-eight! Which meant that out of hundred women who had sex, two would get pregnant using a condom. But surely that meant two people who were ultra-fertile, right? Not people like her, with damaged insides and only one ovary.

No, this had to be exhaustion, or stress, or...

Her mind went blank, only focusing on one thing. Well, there was an easy way to test her theory, wasn't there? But she didn't want to do it. Because she knew that if she did pee on a stick she would begin to hope that a miracle *had* happened, and when it turned negative—which it most definitely would—then she would only experience that crushing disappointment and loss all over again. And she didn't want to go through that.

No. I'm not going to do it. Whatever I'm feeling will pass. I'm sure it's exhaustion and dehydration and low blood sugar. That's all it can be. It will pass. I will not get my hopes up.

Besides, getting pregnant by Henry was not the way she wanted to start a family. He was a man who had only been after a one-night stand. He wouldn't be interested in her in any other way. He'd told her. And she'd told him the same. Her dream was to be married and in love before starting a family, and as she didn't feel able to trust any man right now, getting pregnant from a one-night stand was not how she was going to do things.

No. This isn't happening. I won't allow it to happen. I'm just tired.

'Oh, hey, Natalie! Glad I caught you. I've brought in a couple of books—'

She turned to look at Henry, tears in her eyes. He was always around. It was as if she couldn't go anywhere in this place without running into him. And she didn't want him to see her this way. Confused. Frightened. Feeling ill. Emotional.

And now she was having these stupid ideas about being pregnant just because she'd slept with him. It was ridiculous! She was overreacting. She had to remember she'd been through a lot lately. Not just with everything that had happened with Wade, but with moving away from her home and her family.

New jobs were stressful enough as it was. Learning new systems, having to remember everyone's names, learning new protocols, understanding the hierarchy and politics of a place. She didn't also need to have to avoid the hot attending she'd slept with! Who was being, oh, so mature and kind and considerate, bringing her drinks and books, making her wish for a second night, maybe a third. But she knew that she couldn't, and...

'Are you okay?'

The concern in his eyes was genuine.

She sniffed. Smiled. 'I'm fine! Honestly. Ignore me.'

There was a pause. A hesitation. A look of doubt in his eyes, and then, 'I could never do that.'

He stepped towards her, took her hand in his. A simple gesture? An overture of friendliness? Or was it something more?

She looked at him. What did he mean? Her hand felt electrified by his touch and she didn't want to remove it.

'No?'

Her parents had used to ignore her quite easily. And Wade had taken her for granted. Dropping her the instant his secret was revealed and ignoring her calls from the hospital as she lay in bed, hooked up to drips and machines.

'No. Sit down with me. You look like you need a moment.'

He took her arm, gently guided her towards a couch, then sat down next to her. The concern in his eyes was so intense she almost didn't know how to deal with it.

In his other hand were a couple of books, which he set down on the low coffee table.

'For me?' she asked.

He smiled. 'I thought you might like them.'

She eyed the small pile, noting the authors and titles. They were definitely the kind of books she'd like. And he'd thought about her... brought them in for her. That was so thoughtful.

'You're a very kind man, aren't you, Henry Locke?'

'I try to be.'

'Of course you are. I mean, you save babies. How could a man who saves babies be anything but kind and lovely?'

He frowned, as if he wasn't sure how to answer her question.

'Sorry. As I said, ignore me. I'm feeling emotional. You don't have to stay with me if you're busy. I'll be fine on my own.'

She looked at his profile. Studied his features intently, wondering what it might be like to have made a baby with this man. Silly idea, though. She was letting her mind run away with her. Her brain was stubbornly refusing to accept the truth of her situation. She would probably never get pregnant without help, so why was she allowing herself to imagine and hope?

'Do you want to talk about it?' he asked. 'About what's bothering you? I'm a good listener. I may not be able to help, but I'm a good listener.'

She smiled. 'You're sweet…but I have a patient waiting for me, and if I ever got started on all my issues we'd be here all year,' she tried to joke as she got to her feet. 'Thank you for the books. I look forward to reading them.'

She laid her hand on his shoulder as a gesture of thanks and then she walked away, heart thudding, telling herself that walking away was the best thing to do.

All too easily she allowed herself to fall for men who were nice to her. It was pathetic, really! Was she so starved of affection that she'd done this to herself? Wishing and hoping that maybe Henry was different from Wade?

In the doorway, she turned and looked back at him.

He was watching her still, concern etched deeply across his features.

He really does care. Doesn't he?

'Let's meet up later,' he said. 'When you've got a break.'

'Why?'

He smiled. 'No reason. We'll go for a walk. Shoot the breeze, as you Americans say.'

She nodded. Spending time with him always

made her feel better. His simple gaze acceler-
ated her pulse. His touch could make her feel
so alive. The rest of the time she wondered if
she simply walked around like a zombie.

But for now she had a patient waiting. 'I'll
page you when I'm free.'

CHAPTER FOUR

HENRY SAT IN the staff room, looking down at the two paperbacks he'd brought in and wondering what Natalie's tears had been about.

Seeing her so upset had pained him, and he'd realised with a sudden shock that he couldn't bear it and wanted to make her feel better.

Henry walked over to her locker and placed the books down in front of it. He scribbled on a piece of paper:

I don't need these back.

He signed it with an H. For a moment, he briefly contemplated whether to add a kiss, but decided against it. Because other staff members might see it and start the gossip going, however innocently. And he didn't like to be talked about at work. Not like that, anyway. Not about his private life. That was why he'd never told anyone about Jenny.

Jenny had struggled with her emotions. He'd often found her crying. But whenever he'd tried to help she'd lashed out at him, or yelled, or told him to go away, leaving him feeling helpless. And hopeless. Feeling that everything was going wrong and there was nothing he could do to stop it.

Seeing Natalie cry had reopened that memory box, but instead of brushing him off she had welcomed his touch. Had been grateful for his offer of a listening ear. It had made him feel bold. That he could be there for her even if he couldn't have been there for his wife.

He couldn't bear to witness another woman falling apart. So he vowed, there and then, to help her as much as he could. Even if it was just to listen.

Maybe it would heal them both?

'Okay, Shruti, you need to push, okay?'

'I can't! I'm too tired!' Shruti cried.

Her husband, Kamal, pressed his forehead to his wife's and said something low in Hindi.

'You can. I believe in you,' said Natalie. 'Now's the time to dig deep and get this baby born.'

There were some late decels in the baby's heart rate with every contraction. Each time Shruti bore down the baby's heartrate dropped dramatically. If she wasn't able to push him out soon, then they'd have to go to the OR.

The attending, Dr Serena Chatwin, sat positioned between Shruti's legs, which were up in stirrups. She'd already got forceps placed and was helping Shruti with her pushing.

'One last big push and we can get the head out. We're going to do this together, you and I.'

Shruti nodded, face contorted in pain.

Natalie felt for her. She and Kamal had had such a long journey to getting the baby they had wanted for so long, and she knew that her patient must feel as if she was failing at the final hurdle. But Natalie knew her patient had the strength in her. Every woman did. She just had to believe that she could find it.

'Shruti? Remember all those dreams you had of having your own baby? All that trying? All the upset you went through. That's behind you now. Because right at this minute your precious, much-loved and much-wanted baby is right there, waiting to be born. It's up to you now. One big push and you'll be able to hold your baby in your arms and shower him or her with all the love you've been waiting to share. One big push is all you need. So when that next contraction comes, I want you to take the biggest breath you've taken all day and give it your all. Can you do that?'

Shruti listened and nodded, a look of grim determination settling upon her face. 'It's coming now.'

'Okay.' Natalie looked down at Serena and nodded.

Her patient sucked in a deep breath and pushed hard, and the baby's head finally got around that difficult corner and began to crown.

'Okay, little pushes…little pushes and pant!' ordered Serena.

Shruti breathed heavily in and out as Serena un-looped the umbilical cord from around the baby's neck. It was no wonder those decels had occurred. Every time the mom had pushed, the cord had tightened. But now the baby was free, and he slithered out almost on his own.

'It's a boy!' cried Kamal, cradling his wife's face as Serena laid the newborn baby boy on Shruti's stomach, before clamping the cord and cutting it.

'You did it! Well done!' cried Natalie, beaming with pride and staring down at the new life.

It was a life that this couple had been told would never be possible without help, and look at what they'd achieved. Medicine didn't always know the answers and there *were* miracles. And now this lovely couple had finally achieved their dream of becoming a family.

A dream that Natalie knew would never

come true for her, because she didn't see how she'd be able to trust someone enough. Yes, still she wanted that romantic ideal of marriage and a family. But Wade had set her back with his lies and deceit. She'd believed him to be head over heels in love with her. How could she trust anyone else?

She helped dry off the baby, then positioned Shruti's precious son to begin breastfeeding after she'd run all the checks and measurements on him. Then she left the family to settle, before she moved them to a post-delivery room.

She met Henry in the hospital grounds, over by the memorial garden. It was a small, green area, laid with pathways, interspersed with bushes and flowers, and even a small goldfish pond protected by fencing.

'I…er…wanted to apologise. About earlier.'

'You have nothing to apologise for,' he said.

'I know… I just…' She blushed as she looked up into his face, staring into his eyes as he stared back at her, feeling so many feelings right now she wasn't sure how to react.

Henry might genuinely be the first man ever to see her for who she was. She had been intimate with him and he had seen her body, had not been appalled by its myriad of scars— had, in fact, been delighted by her body. Had brought her to the heights of ecstasies she had only dreamed of.

But he'd been more than that. Had done more for her than that.

He hadn't ignored her. Or taken her for granted.

'I'm not used to being *seen*...' she began, not sure how to explain her complex life and history to this man in one short moment, but knowing that she wanted to at least try. Her emotions were all over the place just lately. 'And I just feel that...that you *do* see me. And not because you want to use me, or take advantage of me, the way men have done to me in the past. You seem genuine, and kind, and I wanted to say that...' She looked once again into the beautiful blue of his eyes. 'That I see you, too. And so far... I like what I see. So, thank you. Again.'

She laughed nervously, wondering just what the hell she was doing, spilling out her feelings like this. Randomly, in the hospital garden. This was different from the flirting they'd been doing. This was serious stuff.

'I don't normally get emotional,' she went on. 'I was just feeling a bit weird and you caught me at a vulnerable moment. I didn't want you to think I was crazy!' Another laugh. Embarrassed. Nervous.

He was smiling at her. 'You're not crazy by any means.'

They came across a bench and Henry indicated that they should sit down. She felt nervous suddenly. She had no idea what was going on in her body and, yes, of course she could just be imagining the whole thing. But what if she *was* pregnant? And this man was the father? He'd been a fabulous one-night stand, and a great flirty friend, and an amazing colleague— but did that make him good father material? Or would he abandon her as Wade had done?

'Well, I appreciate you saying that.'

'Easy to say when it's true. I know our relationship didn't start off in the most conventional way, and that we've both…felt things… but I am here for you. If you're homesick, or whatever it is that's bothering you.'

He thought she was homesick. Okay. She could run with that for now. 'It has been bothering me. Being away from home, not having anyone to lean on.'

'You can lean on me,' he said.

And she could tell that he meant it.

'You're sweet,' she replied, and impulsively she leaned over and pressed a soft kiss to his cheek, before getting up and hurrying away, feeling his eyes upon her the whole time.

She headed to the cafeteria to grab some

lunch. She felt as if she was fizzing after her chat with Henry…full of nervous energy. She breezed past most of the sandwiches, craving something with a bit of a kick, and selected some chilli and rice.

As she sat at the table the aroma made her mouth water, and the chilli itself, when she tasted it, was awesome! Not mild at all, but with quite a kick to it. She wolfed it down, sad when it was gone too soon, and wondering if the café assistants would think her a pig if she went back for a second helping?

She sat staring the food counters, tapping her foot rapidly against the floor…deciding. Deciding it didn't matter what the assistants thought. She got up to re-join the queue, but as soon as she'd stood and begun to take a few steps realised that she'd begun to feel decidedly queasy.

Maybe I've eaten too fast?

She began to hiccup, with each lurch of her stomach making her feel worse, and knew she had to get to a bathroom. There was one just outside the cafeteria doors, and she raced into it and opened the nearest stall and threw up her lunch.

Afterwards, she felt marginally better.

Was the chilli off? Or was it too spicy? Or could this possibly be what I'm terrified of it being?

Pregnant. That was what she was scared of the most. And yet at the same time it was what she wanted most in the entire world, and that was why she was scared to admit it. To take a test and see.

Because if she was, then it wasn't the right time. This wasn't how she wanted to have a child. A child should be conceived in love, not from a one-night stand. Although, doing the job she did, she saw plenty of babies who'd originated that way.

Because if she was, then her whole world would turn upside down.

Because if she *wasn't*, then she would have allowed her hopes back in and that was a difficult box to close again.

At the sinks, she rinsed her mouth out with water and stared at her reflection. She looked tired. Exhausted, even. A bit green about the gills. She shook her head, telling herself she was being stupid even to consider that she might be pregnant with Henry's baby. But she knew she had to take a test to find out.

She felt bad about taking one of the tests from work. She felt she ought to buy her own from a pharmacy on the way home. But she knew she couldn't wait until then. She needed to know *now.* Needed to see that it was actually negative so she could forget all this mental turmoil about whether she was or not. And when she *wasn't* she'd know she had a bug, or something. She'd stay at home. Let it pass. Then return to work feeling better and brighter and move on with her life.

She and Henry were in a good place right now. As long as he didn't think she was a nut-job because one minute she'd been crying and the next smiling and kissing him on the cheek.

She sneaked into a bathroom on the delivery floor with her test and, taking a deep breath, peed on the stick. She placed it on the toilet cistern and turned her back on it.

I can't believe I'm feeling so scared!

She knew it would say negative. But a tiny part of her—the part that had been devastated when that doctor had sat on her bed and told her it was unlikely she'd ever have children naturally—wanted it to be positive. Because... Well, she didn't know why. To show the doctors that they were wrong? To have the child she'd always craved?

Because having a child with Henry would be...

She wanted to think it would be good.

But she was terrified, too. If it *was* positive, then her whole life would be on a new trajectory—and not in the most ideal circumstances. Her parents were very traditional in their views and believed in marriage before kids. Would they be angry with her? And what about Henry? He'd made it clear he wasn't interested in a relationship, even if he *had* said he would be there for her. That she could lean on him.

But he'd meant as a friend, right?

She checked her fob watch. A minute had gone by. Too early to look…

But she couldn't resist. So she leaned forward to grab it and closed her eyes, stood up straight and steadied her breathing. Until she felt ready to look.

And then she opened her eyes.

Two lines. Two very strong pink lines.

Pregnant!

Natalie gasped and sank to her knees, her back sliding down the stall door as she stared in shock at the test before her. She was pregnant with Henry's baby! Pregnant! With a baby naturally conceived, despite her injuries, despite using protection! How was that even possible?

Life finds a way.

Her mother had said that when she'd heard the news that Natalie probably wouldn't have a child of her own. She'd clutched the cross at her neck and told her that if it was meant to be then life would find a way.

At the time, she'd thought it was just her

mother, clinging desperately to her religion and her belief in God, believing that somehow the Lord would one day provide her daughter with the family she so desperately wanted. That she was saying it just in reassurance, because she wasn't sure she believed it. But wanted to offer her hope.

And somehow her prayers had come true.

'I'm pregnant...' she whispered to herself out loud, needing to hear the words. To make it seem more real.

The temptation to do another test, just to make sure she hadn't had a false positive, was strong. But she knew she didn't dare take another test from the hospital stores. She would buy one on the way home.

But what was she supposed to do now?

All her symptoms added up, but was she supposed to just come out of the stall and return to work as normal, without saying a word to anyone? Her whole life had just changed in an instant! A major event had blown the wind from her sails and yet she was expected to behave normally.

What else am I meant to do?

Her 'glass half empty' nature told her she was still very much in the early, dangerous days of the first trimester, and with her internal injuries she had no idea if the pregnancy would remain viable anyway. She could miscarry. She could lose it. What was the point in telling people and going through all the upset and turmoil if that was going to happen anyway?

So…no. She'd keep it to herself. Especially from Henry. Henry seemed the kind of guy who would do the right thing. But how did she really know? And what would be the point in telling him if she was just going to lose it?

For now, she decided, she'd keep it to herself.

Three separate pregnancy tests had sat on the kitchen counter earlier that morning and all of them were positive. There was no mistaking it.

Natalie had simply stared at them for a while before heading into work, mind blown, utterly unable to comprehend the news, still feeling numb when she bumped into Henry as he arrived on his bike.

'Morning. You okay? You look like you've seen a ghost,' he joked.

She was going to be a mother. In a few months. Unless the world did what it usually did and went all to hell.

'I didn't get much sleep last night, that's all.'
I'll need to get some folic acid.

The pregnancy probably wouldn't last anyway. First pregnancies often ended in miscarriage, but for the time she was pregnant she needed to do her absolute best in keeping healthy. Just in case.

Just in case I go full term.

'Did you see the news?'

She blinked. 'What news?'

'The lady on TV? Giving birth to her own grandchildren? Fifty-seven years of age and being a surrogate for her daughter. Now that's one hell of a surprise, huh?'

I've had my own surprise.

'Surprise pregnancies? Yeah.' She smiled weakly, waiting for him to finish locking up his bike.

For so long she'd been the midwife. And now, possibly, she would be the patient. The aspiring mother-to-be on the bed. If she made it to full term, who would be her birth partner? Her mom? Henry? Who knew? The first would be extremely disapproving of her having a child out of wedlock, and the other... Well, she didn't know enough about the other, truth be told. But she felt he would offer to be there. He seemed gentlemanly. He seemed as if he would want to do the right thing. But...

I've been so wrong about men before and look what happened to me!

And if the pregnancy did last? Where would she live? The apartment she rented was a shoebox, the cheapest she could find. She couldn't raise a baby in that place.

'I couldn't imagine my mother carrying my baby, could you?'

'Your mother? No.'

But could you imagine me?

They were all gathered together for the morning handover from night shift. Henry stood at the back of the room and became acutely aware of Natalie's presence the second she entered, with only minutes to spare. He watched her edge her way through to a spare seat. Saw the way she tucked a stray curl back behind her ear. The way she smiled at someone who moved their legs to one side, so she could pass and sit down.

He thought of the kiss she'd given him yesterday. How her lips had felt against his cheek. How it had made him feel. How he had felt running into her this morning, hoping no one noticed how he looked at her. Hoping no one registered his growing feelings for Natalie upon his face. He was concerned, though. She looked pale. Tired. He glanced back, concerned for her, worrying, hoping that she wasn't ill, and let himself gaze at her in what he hoped was an unobtrusive way.

The handover began and he started scribbling notes on his notepad, as he always did when he received the updates for his patients. He didn't like to miss anything. He wanted to know if there'd been any changes overnight. Any test results that might have come in.

Dr Yang was speaking. '...and I've got a macrosomia case that's been transferred over from Queen's. Baby is already weighing in at about ten pounds. Could be a complicated delivery. So, I'll need a midwife. Any volunteers?'

Natalie raised her hand.

'Thank you, Nurse Webber. And I'd like you, Dr Locke, to assist me with that case.'

Henry nodded, glancing at Natalie, who'd turned to look at him. Now, what *was* that expression in her eyes? Concern? Was she worrying about how he'd be with her after yesterday's kiss? Even if it had been only on his cheek?

The case was interesting. Foetal macrosomia meant a baby that was considered much larger than average. It could be caused by gestational diabetes in the mother, or simply excessive weight gain, but the delivery could be complicated by uterine atony—where the womb didn't contract after birth, so there would be heavy postnatal bleeding.

At that moment Dr Yang's phone sounded and he glanced at it. 'Our case is here. Natalie? Henry? Shall we?'

Henry excused himself as he sidled past his colleagues, and then waited politely for Natalie to leave the room first, so he could follow.

Ahead of them, Dr Yang strode down the corridor, his step brisk, stopping only to check at the desk on which room his patient had been put in.

'Room Seventeen, people! Now, let's remember, Mom is scared. She's away from her home base and has no one to support her. Nurse Webber? I'd like you to try and make her feel as comfortable as you can—understood?'

Natalie nodded. 'Yes.'

'Okay. Let's go.'

Dr Yang opened the door to the room and strode in as if he owned the place. He was clearly the king of this department, and all the staff and patients were his subjects, whom he was honouring with his presence.

'Hello, Lakeisha, my name is Dr Yang, and these are my colleagues, Dr Locke and Nurse Webber. Now, we're all here to take care of you and get you through the next hour or so.' He smiled and turned to Henry. 'Can you present the case, please?' He passed over the notes.

Henry flipped open the file. 'Lakeisha Waring, twenty-four years of age, thirty-nine weeks and three days pregnant with her first child. Strep B negative. Normal first pregnancy otherwise, fundus measurements always measuring high, no excessive amniotic fluid reported, current weight estimate of just over ten pounds.'

He smiled at Lakeisha when he finished.

She gave a small clap. 'Marvellous, Doctor. You've done your bit—now let me do mine.' She stuck mouthpiece delivering the nitrous oxide to her lips and began to suck on it as her contraction built.

She was already attached to a CTG machine and Natalie stepped forward to check it. 'No visible decels. Baby is coping well, it seems.'

Dr Yang smiled like a proud father as he turned to talk to Henry. 'I'd like you and Natalie to stay with Lakeisha and monitor her until she gets to ten centimetres. Then call me immediately—understood?'

'Yes, sir.'

Yang waited until Lakeisha had finished her contraction. 'I'm going to leave you in my trusted colleagues' capable hands, but I'll be back for the big finish, so you just relax and let us take care of everything, okay?'

And then he swept from the room.

Lakeisha looked at Henry and Natalie with surprise. 'Did that dude just tell me to *relax*? With a ten-pound baby about to burst from my vajayjay?'

Natalie nodded, smiling. 'He did.'

'I'll give him *relax*.' Then she began to huff and puff again, as another contraction began.

Natalie looked at Henry, hesitantly, holding out her hand for the notes.

He passed them over. 'I ought to examine her,' he said.

'Okay.'

'Could you do a basic set of obs? Get her BP and temperature for me?'

'Sure.'

There was definitely something happening between them, although he was completely unsure what. He liked being in Natalie's company, and often found himself seeking her out. Looking for her.

He waited for Lakeisha's contraction to be over. 'I need to examine you, if that's okay?'

'As long as you're gentler than the last lot. I felt like a side of meat.'

'I'll try. But if things get uncomfortable you just let me know and I'll stop, okay?'

'*Relax? Uncomfortable?* You guys sure don't know how this feels.' Lakeisha turned to Natalie. 'Do you think we'd tell guys to 'relax' if they had ten-pound babies coming out of their wazoo?'

Natalie laughed as she wrapped a blood pressure cuff around their patient's right arm. 'I hope so!'

'I don't think so. I think if guys had the babies they'd have found a different way, believe you me.' She grimaced as Henry began his examination.

'Sorry. Just a moment longer… Yep, you're about nine centimetres.' He removed his glove, discarding it in the clinical wastebin, then washed his hands. 'How are you feeling?'

'How do you expect?'

He smiled. 'You're in the best place. Anyone coming to hold your hand, or…?'

'No. The father made a run for it the second I got pregnant again.'

'What about your family, Lakeisha?' Natalie asked.

'They're at home. Covid.'

'Oh, I'm sorry. Well, I guess Henry and I will have to do.'

'Never thought I'd give birth with only strangers here.'

Natalie smiled. 'Well, we'll introduce ourselves a bit more, so we're friends, not strangers.' She turned to look at Henry, and he saw there was some colour back in her cheeks, mischief on her face. 'You go first. Tell Lakeisha all about yourself.'

Ah… He could see what she was doing. This wasn't about letting Lakeisha feel she wasn't with strangers—this was about Natalie trying to find out more about him. He smiled at her, but he never gave out too much personal detail at work. He always kept the details he did give trivial.

He turned to smile at Lakeisha. 'I'm Henry. Originally from Oxford, England. I have a brother called Hugh, who was over here recently, but he's gone back to the UK now. My father was in the marines and my mother was a nurse—which is where I get my love of medicine. I guess you could say I'm an introvert. I like music and books. Dog person, rather than cats, though I like both. I prefer dark chocolate to milk, strawberry milkshakes over vanilla, and my favourite ice cream is mint choc chip.'

He glanced at Natalie with a special smile, to show her that he'd cleverly evaded her probing.

Natalie narrowed her eyes at him, pursing her lips with amusement. 'I'm Natalie. I just came to New York after living my entire life in a small town in Montana.'

'Whereabouts?' asked Lakeisha. 'I've always wanted to go the country.'

'Near Scobey? Heard of it?'

Their patient shook her head and then began to suck again on the nitrous oxide.

'I don't like crowds or busy places,' Natalie went on. 'I miss the hills and the animals we had on our farm. I miss my family and my best friend, Gayle. I miss my dog. I like to dance when no one is watching. I sing in the shower because that's the only place my voice sounds great.' She laughed, placing a hand on her belly as if she was hungry. 'And my favourite ice cream is rocky road.'

'Okay, my turn.' Now that the contraction was over, Lakeisha seemed better able to talk. 'I'm Lakeisha. I'm about to have an amazing son. I fall for all the wrong guys and make terrible decisions. I love to eat dip and salsa and salted popcorn, which explains my waistline even when I'm not pregnant. I don't like sweet things at all and…' she breathed in '…and I think you're gonna need to pass me a bowl or something. Because I'm gonna puke!'

Natalie hurriedly passed a long blue bag that looked like a sock to Lakeisha, who groaned and held it close to her mouth, but didn't vomit.

'Why do I feel this way?'

'Could be transition,' suggested Henry.

'Oh. Delightful.' Lakeisha lay her head back against the pillow, still clutching the blue bag. 'I'll keep this, if you don't mind?'

'Be our guest.' Henry smiled and went to stand with Natalie. 'You have a dog?' he said.

She smiled at him. 'Back home, yes.'

'What breed is he?'

'He's just a mongrel. Nothing special.'

'All dogs are special.'

'You ever think of getting one yourself?'

'One day, maybe. But not now. It'd be wrong to work this many hours and leave it home alone, or in doggy daycare.'

'Perhaps one day when you settle down and have kids?' Natalie asked.

She was probing again. He could hear it in the tone of her voice. She was asking if he saw that in his future one day. He had to admit that for some reason he liked her asking these questions. He was enjoying the fact that she wanted to know more about him. It proved that they'd been more than just one crazy night.

'Maybe. One day.'

He'd never rule that option out. But he didn't see it happening for a long while.

His eyes fell upon the trace. It was still looking good, though there were early signs of the baby's heartbeat dipping with each contraction. Nothing too significant, but enough to make him think that maybe the baby was tiring of labour.

'How long have you been contracting?' he asked Lakeisha.

'Half a day.'

'Everything okay?' Natalie asked in a whisper beside him.

It was difficult having her this close. Close

enough to touch. But he couldn't let it unsettle him. Despite the fact that just being near to her gave him the urge to reach out and touch her. It would be enough to just touch her arm. Her hand. Her cheek…

'Baby's tiring,' he said.

Lakeisha was beginning to tremble, her whole body shaking. 'What's happening?'

Henry stepped away from Natalie's proximity. 'Trembling like this is normal…don't worry. It's your body in transition.'

'F-f-fun,' she said, teeth chattering.

Natalie took her hand. 'You're going to be fine.'

'Tell that to my vajayjay.'

Henry smiled. 'I'm just going to have Dr Yang paged. I'll be back in a moment.'

Outside in the corridor, he felt as if he could breathe again. That moment, standing so close to Natalie and breathing in her scent, had been like torture. A terrible yet delicious and tempting torture. His senses had gone into overload, his body reacting to her and needing her desperately, like an addict craving a hit. Stepping away and trying to pretend that everything was normal had been agony.

'Page Dr Yang to Lakeisha Waring's room, please,' he asked Roxy, who was on the desk.

'Sure thing. Hey, you're in with Nat, right?'

He nodded. 'Yes?'

'Is she okay?'

'I think so. Why?'

'I don't know… I thought she looked a little tired today.'

'I think you're describing every hospital employee on this planet.'

Roxy laughed. 'Ain't that the truth?' she said as she picked up the phone to page Dr Yang.

Henry headed back to the room.

'She's feeling the urge to push.'

That was what Natalie greeted him with, the second he walked through the door.

'Great, I'll get ready.'

Henry checked his trolley, to make sure he had all the sterile packs and equipment he'd need, and got gowned up as Natalie began guiding Lakeisha through how to push. This was her first try at delivering vaginally.

Behind him, Dr Yang knocked and then entered the room. 'All systems go, I hear?'

'Yes, sir.'

Dr Yang stood for a moment and watched Lakeisha pushing to judge the quality of it. 'You're doing excellently, Ms Waring.'

Lakeisha gasped for air. 'I'm so glad you approve!'

Dr Yang examined the trace and then moved

to stand next to Henry. 'Baby is getting tired,' he said in a low voice.

'I know.'

'I say we give her half an hour to try and do this herself and after that we intervene—unless that trace tells us otherwise.'

'Agreed.'

Dr Yang turned back to Lakeisha. 'Okay, with these next contractions I really need you to push as hard as you can.'

'What do you *think* I'm doing?' Lakeisha yelled.

'I think you're doing great, but I know you can do better. This is a big boy, so it's going to take you some enormous effort to push him out,' answered Dr Yang in his normal, no-nonsense, let's-just-get-on-with-this voice.

'Is he okay?'

'He's doing fine, but he's getting tired. It's showing on the trace.'

Lakeisha nodded silently and frowned, and Natalie proffered her a small sip of water.

Dr Yang began to glove and gown up, standing behind Henry, who had seated himself between the stirrups and was checking baby's station and position.

'Okay, good… He's face down, just as we want him. He's doing his part—now we need you to do yours.'

Lakeisha sucked in a breath and began to bear down, grimacing with the effort of pushing hard. Clearly she no longer had time to make jokes with them and meant business.

Dr Yang looked on.

This was a large baby, but Henry really thought she could do it. It was possible. The largest baby Henry had ever seen born vaginally had been nearly eleven pounds, and though there'd been a bad second-degree tear, there'd been no awful complications.

But still he was alert, as he always was, ready to leap into action if needed. And he knew they could act fast, if it was required.

They could see the top of the baby's head now, and it was thick with dark hair.

'You're doing well, Lakeisha! Baby's right there. Keep pushing hard.'

'I'm *trying*!'

Dr Yang went over to Natalie. 'I'll take over coaching. Can you get the NICU staff paged—stat? Just to be on the safe side?'

She nodded.

Dr Yang dampened a cloth and wiped Lakeisha's face. 'Okay, another breath and then bear right down into your bottom. One...two...three...'

Henry looked up from his place between the

stirrups and with a look asked Dr Yang to check the trace.

He watched as he checked the peaks and troughs and saw that the baby was not coping with the delivery at all well now.

Dr Yang turned back to Henry and gave him another practised look that said, *We need to get this baby out—stat.*

'Okay, Ms Waring, your baby is getting tired and I think you need some help. I can use a ventouse, which is a suction cup placed on the baby's head that I can use to help pull him out as you push.'

'Do it!'

Henry placed the cup, but after a few tries it was clear it wasn't working.

'Okay, change of plan to forceps,' said Dr Yang. 'And I may need to make a small cut to help facilitate his birth.'

'I don't care—just get him out!'

Natalie returned to the room with the NICU team, who checked the prepped warmer and the oxygen and then stood behind Henry, ready to take the baby when he arrived.

Henry made the cut after injecting a dose of local anaesthetic, and then positioned the forceps around the baby's head. 'Next big push we need to get the head out, okay?'

'Okay.'

Lakeisha's face filled with a determination that was very familiar to Henry and to most OBGYNs. It was the look of a woman who had reached a wall and had decided that even if the wall might try to stop her she was going to power on through it anyway. Because her baby was at stake and Mother Bears would do anything to help their babies. She was tired, and she was hurting, and she was vulnerable and alone, but still she would find the strength somewhere—even if it took her own last breath to do so.

She sucked in a huge lungful of air, scrunched her face up tight and began to push, a growl straining from her throat and her teeth clenched, her face a mask of pain and exhaustion, yet also filled with determination and good old-fashioned gumption.

And it was working! Baby's head had come out.

Henry quickly discarded the forceps and used his hands to help manoeuvre the shoulders, and then baby was out. Big and floppy, and totally done in by the shock of the birth.

Henry swiftly handed the baby boy over to the NICU team, who surrounded him in an instant and got to work.

'Is he okay?' cried Lakeisha.

'They're working on him now,' Natalie said, taking her hand in hers and rubbing it.

But Henry could see her bleeding wouldn't stop. 'Dr Yang?'

Dr Yang tried to feel for the top of Lakeisha's fundus, to help massage the womb down, but it was as they'd feared. Her uterus was atonic and wouldn't shrink back after such a big baby, and neither was the placenta making an appearance. She'd already lost so much blood…

Henry looked up at Lakeisha. 'You've done a brilliant job in getting your son here, but your womb isn't contracting, so we need to get you to the OR.'

'I'm not going until I know my son is okay.'

Natalie bent forward. 'I'll stay with him. I'll sit with him. He won't be alone. You have my word.'

'But…' Lakeisha looked from Natalie to Henry to the team of NICU staff, still gathered around her baby like bees around a flower. 'I need to know he's okay!'

Henry bit his lip. This was one of the hardest parts of his job. He needed to save this mother from bleeding out, but that wasn't her priority at this moment. She needed to know her baby was all right.

'Lakeisha? I understand you want to put your baby first—I get that. But if we don't get this bleeding stopped then you might be too sick to look after him. If you want to look after him, then you've also got to take care of yourself.'

Lakeisha looked at him, paling.

But luckily, at that moment, her baby let out a small cry.

Lakeisha sobbed, her hand suddenly covering her mouth. 'He's okay?'

'He was struggling to breathe, but we've got him,' said someone from the NICU team.

'All right, Doctor. Do what you have to do. You promise you'll stay with him?' Lakeisha asked Natalie.

'Every second until you're back from the OR,' she promised.

'Okay…'

'Okay, let's go!'

Henry and Dr Yang began to roll the bed from the room and rushed their patient straight through to the OR, leaving Natalie and the baby behind.

CHAPTER FIVE

LAKEISHA'S BABY HAD been stunned and exhausted by the birth process. It happened. And, although it happened frequently, it wasn't a situation that the staff took calmly. Their absolute focus was on those babies. Warming them. Drying them. Giving them oxygen. Trying to stimulate them into taking a breath.

Baby Waring did breathe on his own, but that minute in which he hadn't shown any response at all had been terrifying for all involved.

But now he'd begun to make respiratory effort and everyone breathed a sigh of relief. He lay wrapped in blankets, in Natalie's arms, awaiting the first cuddle with his mother.

Natalie stared down at the baby boy. He'd weighed ten pounds and three ounces, so he was more than a decent size for a newborn! And he was adorable. Thick black curls beneath his blue knitted hat. Chubby cheeks. A cute button nose. And dark, curious eyes.

She held him in her arms and she wondered…

Wondered about whether she would get through this pregnancy and hold her own child. Wondered about whether this pregnancy was going to be as problematic as all her other relationships. Wondered about Henry and what secrets he might be hiding. But, most of all, what would *her* baby look like?

She'd never allowed herself to think about it at all. Why put herself through such torture? Why waste hours dreaming about something she'd never thought she'd have. And yet now… Now there was a chance. And she could dream and she could hope and she could be scared. Because having her own baby was something she'd hoped for *so much*!

She was pregnant. She had all the symptoms. Even now the nausea was present, but was being kept in check by the bliss of sitting here, holding a baby in her arms.

What would it feel like to watch her belly grow?

What would it feel like to experience new life kicking and stretching inside her?

'You have a mom who loves you very much,' she whispered. 'And I'm going to be a mommy, too, but don't tell anyone because it's a secret.'

Natalie smiled, because she knew her secret

was safe with him—but also because it was the first time she'd actually said it out loud somewhere other than in the safety of her own apartment.

She suddenly felt so happy. Despite everything. Despite the fact that this wasn't a perfect situation and she wasn't having a child the way she'd hoped to and there would be so much to sort out. Moving. Affording the baby. Taking time off work when it was born. How would she deal with childcare? There was a nursery here at the hospital, for staff members, but was there a waiting list? Did she have to enquire about it now? There was so much she didn't know.

And she couldn't help but think about Henry saying that one day he would get a dog. One day he would settle down and have a family. He did dream of it. At least he'd said so, anyway. But she was firmly still in the friend zone.

'Problems for another day,' she told the baby. 'But not today. Let's just get you reunited with your momma, huh?'

Natalie heard footsteps and looked up, seeing Henry dressed in scrubs coming towards her. It appeared that Henry was one of those lucky people who looked good in anything. Clothes. Scrubs. Naked…

She felt her cheeks bloom at the thought, and then a sudden bolt of lust hit her low in the gut.

She began to tingle, feeling her body respond at the thought of him.

He pulled off his scrub cap and gave her a quick smile. 'How's the baby doing?'

'He's doing brilliantly after his slow start. How's Lakeisha?'

He grimaced. 'We couldn't stop the bleeding. We had to do an emergency hysterectomy.'

'Oh no! Poor Lakeisha.' She knew he'd be feeling really sad about that. No doctor liked to make that choice in surgery, but if they had no other option, then that was what they had to do.

But to hear that kind of news…she knew what it had felt like to be told she might not be able to have children and that had hurt like hell, but to know for sure? To know that your womb had been removed…

'I'd like you in there with me when we tell her. I feel we have a bond with her, and it will do her good to have familiar faces there.'

'Okay.' She stood up to put the baby back in his crib. 'Is she in Recovery?'

'Yes, she's awake, but a little groggy still.'

Natalie tucked baby Waring under his blankets and began to wheel him to Recovery with Henry by her side. She felt a little awkward. Knowing she was keeping this secret from him, fighting her physical craving for him. It was as if all her wiring inside had been mixed up by an amateur and parts of her were firing on all cylinders, when clearly it was inappropriate right now to be wanting to tear Henry's clothes off and take him like an animal in the linen cupboard, whispering her secret into his ear.

She risked a side-glance at him. 'I didn't know that your mother was a nurse.'

Henry nodded. 'Yes, she was.'

'What kind?' she persisted, knowing she could never walk in silence with him. She needed to talk to him. Needed to know what she could about him. To try and work out who he was. To discover his secrets.

'She was a scrub nurse.'

'Oh. I guess she had some tales to tell?'

A faint smile touched his lips. 'A few.'

Natalie stopped, shaking her head and smiling. 'You're really not going to give me anything, are you?'

Henry turned to look at her, clearly enjoying this game between them.

'I want to know about you,' she told him. 'Who you are. What makes you tick.'

'Why?'

He seemed amused, as if he was wanting her to say *Because I'm interested in you.*

'Because I want to know.' She stared at him then, lowering her voice. 'We were intimate. We shared one incredible night and...' She shrugged. 'I just feel like I want to know you better. To understand you. Understand who I got involved with.'

He smiled at her. Did he seem glad that she felt that way? Even though they'd told themselves *not* to get involved? Not to pursue anything with each other.

Maybe he wanted to know more about her, too?

They stopped outside the recovery room's doors.

Henry stared at her so intently she almost wilted beneath his strong gaze. It was as if he was assessing her, deciding internally whether to say any more. She hoped he would give her something. *Anything!* Some iota of information that would help her understand him a little better and decide what kind of man he was.

'Would you like to meet me for a drink?' he asked. 'There's a favourite place I like to go to and I haven't shared it with you yet. Away from here. Just a coffee. Maybe a bite to eat?'

This was it. She knew it. The moment in which she could either decide to plough on alone or accept his invitation and allow herself to get in deeper with this man. The father of her baby.

I don't want to be alone.

'I'd like that.' She blushed as she said it, heat

flooding her face as her stomach rolled with nerves.

He nodded. 'After work?'

'Sure.'

Henry pushed open the recovery bay doors and indicated where Lakeisha was. She looked tired and pale, but most of all relieved that it all seemed to be over.

She perked up at the sight of the crib and a broad smile crept across her face. 'Is that him?'

Natalie beamed. 'It is! All ten pounds and three ounces of him. Do you want to hold him?'

'You bet.'

'Let me prop you up a bit,' Henry suggested, pushing a button on the bed that elevated the back-rest, so that Lakeisha was in a sitting position.

Natalie scooped the baby into her arms, smiling all the time, because this was the best part of her job. Handing a healthy baby over to a healthy mama for the first time.

'Oh, my Lord! He's so precious! He looks like me!' Lakeisha gazed down adoringly at her son.

'Does he have a name?' Natalie asked.

'Kofi. It suits him, don't you think?' asked Lakeisha, examining her son's little fingers.

'It's perfect,' agreed Natalie.

But as she stood there she could feel her nausea coming back in a big way. She needed to get something to eat. One of the ginger cookies she'd brought with her in her bag. Maybe a drink of something tangy, like fresh orange juice.

Perhaps it wasn't the pregnancy sickness. Maybe it was nerves because of the big news they had to tell Lakeisha, about her emergency hysterectomy. That this baby would be the last she'd ever have.

'Lakeisha, you lost a lot of blood after delivery and, as you know, we had to take you into the OR,' Henry said gently.

Lakeisha nodded.

'We did all we could to stop the bleeding, but we were unsuccessful. So, to save you, we had to perform an emergency hysterectomy.'

Natalie watched their patient carefully. She herself knew what it was like to receive such massive news.

'Oh. I see.'

'I can talk you through the surgery, if you'd like? Answer any questions you may have.'

'I can't have any more children?' She looked down at Kofi.

'You won't be able to carry any more babies, no.'

Natalie couldn't bear it. Panicking, she

glanced at Henry. 'Could you...er...excuse me a moment?'

And she quickly left Henry and Lakeisha behind as she hurried to the staff room and her locker, hating herself for leaving Henry so suddenly, in the lurch.

Hurriedly she wolfed down a ginger cookie or two, sighing with relief as they instantly settled her stomach. But her heart was with Lakeisha and what she'd just discovered, and she wanted to tell the world that sometimes miracles happened.

Her hand went to her belly.

Natalie had left so suddenly. One minute she'd been smiling at Lakeisha, gazing adoringly at baby Kofi, and then it was as if a shadow had crossed over her and she'd suddenly made her excuses and left.

It was most definitely odd, and when he found her moments later in the staff room he was really beginning to get concerned. 'You okay?'

'Fine.' She stared back. 'Just tired, you know?'

He felt it must be more than that. She'd seemed terribly upset at hearing they'd performed an emergency hysterectomy on Lakeisha. Almost like it was *personal* news. He thought back to their night together. To her scars. She'd had hip surgery, that was clear. But there'd been other marks. Laparoscopy scars. And a jagged silver line across her pelvis.

A car accident, she'd said. But what if it was more than that? Could Natalie not have children? Was that what this was all about?

'If you don't want to go for that coffee later, we can postpone to another time.'

She looked up at him. 'No. I still want to go.' She managed a smile.

'You're sure? I don't want to push you into anything.'

'No. It'll be good to talk. Away from the hospital.'

He nodded. 'Okay. I'll pick you up later.'

The Central Park Café was situated on the northeast side of Central Park. It was small, intimate, yet busy, with servers busy attending tables, delivering trays of drinks and pastries, as well as a long queue at the counter that led out through the door, of people popping in to get takeout orders.

'We certainly got here at the right time,' Natalie said, as Henry pulled out a chair for her by the window so that she could sit down.

He smiled. 'It helps to book a table. I rang ahead, because I knew it would be busy. It always is.'

Natalie looked a lot better this evening. There was a bit more colour in her cheeks and her eyes were bright. It was incredibly strange, seeing her in casual clothes and not her CNM uniform. She wore an off-the-shoulder white top, that was slightly cropped, and black jeans with some boat shoes. A messenger bag was strapped across her chest.

She lifted it off and hung it from the back of her seat. 'Do you come here often?' she asked, before shaking her head and laughing. 'I can't believe I just asked that.'

He liked it. 'Actually, I do. I pass this place most mornings when I cycle in, and if it's not too busy pop in for one of their breakfast sandwiches.'

A server welcomed them and handed them a menu. 'I'll come take your drink order in just a moment.' And then she disappeared to clear a table.

Natalie perused the menu with enthusiasm. 'I hope they've got something good. I'm starving!'

'Good. Pick anything. My treat.'

She smiled at him over the top of the menu. 'Well, aren't you kind? I'll have a decaf latte and their spiced scampi and peppered potato wedges.'

'Sounds great. I'll join you.'

They put their menus down, gave the server their order and then turned their attention to each other.

'So, how are you?' he asked.

'I'm good.'

'I'm glad to hear it. Lakeisha's case was difficult.'

Natalie glanced out of the window at a mother pushing her child along in a stroller. 'Some cases just get to me, that's all. I like Lakeisha. She's great. It's just that I know what a battle she's got ahead of her.'

'Her recovery, you mean?'

'More the mental and emotional side of things. That was big news you gave her today. I think sometimes we medics give patients news like that and then we walk away to deal with other things. And they're left there, reeling, with no one around to support them.'

'Is that something you've experienced yourself?' he asked softly, leaning in to reach for her hand upon the table. 'You know you can talk to me about *anything*, don't you?'

She smiled, blushing. 'Of course.'

She looked down at their hands and he wondered if he'd imposed on her.

'Were you...?' He paused briefly as the server arrived with their drinks, then when she was gone again looked Natalie in the eyes. 'Were you ever given big news like that?'

Natalie withdrew her hand and looked down and away, out of the window at Central Park. It looked so green and vibrant out there. People were sitting on the grassy areas. Others were on benches, reading books.

'Once upon a time I was, yes.'

'You don't have to talk about it if you don't want to. I just thought I'd let you know that... well, I'm here, if you ever want to.'

She looked at him then with such intensity, such a need to share, that he thought she just might unburden herself. She was considering him, weighing her options, he could tell, and so he sat there, trying to look as open and receptive as he could. He wanted her to share. He wanted to help. He wanted to listen.

He wanted to show her that he could be her friend.

And maybe more?

He'd never felt this way about a woman before, and that was strange. Jenny had outright refused to talk to him about anything, and he'd wondered if he just wasn't cut out for romantic entanglements. That maybe he was faulty in some way. But now Natalie had come along and she had made him wonder. Had made him want to know her deeply.

'There's something about you, Natalie.' He smiled, watching with wonder as the twinkle returned to her eyes at his compliment. 'I don't know what it is, but you make me want to…'

'Want to what?' she asked, taking a sip from her tall latte.

'Makes me want to be with you. All the time. I look for you in the hospital. I can't stop thinking about you. And when I'm with you…' He laughed, because he couldn't quite believe he was sharing these thoughts with her, but was completely unable to do anything to stop himself. 'You make me smile. You terrify me. You make me want to show you that I'm a good guy.'

'Wow,' she said. 'That's nice to hear. So you're a good guy?'

He nodded. 'I'd like to think that maybe I'm one of the best. I save babies' lives, remember?'

'That's right. You do.' She looked back at him, head tilted, a broad smile across her face. And then their food arrived, hot and steaming. 'You inspire me, too.'

'I do?'

That pleased him. He could feel his body's senses coming alive. He wanted to touch her again. Wanted not to have a table between them. To explore her the way he had on New

Year's Eve. Though technically it had been New Year's Day. Very early in the morning!

'Of course. But…'

Ah, the dreaded 'but'.

'But we need to be careful. I think we both have a lot of baggage, and we need to pick through that carefully before we do anything rash.'

'What do you consider "rash"?' he asked, leaning across the table and speaking in a conspiratorial whisper.

He saw her gaze drop to his lips. Saw her take in a breath.

'Something we might both regret.'

They took a walk through Central Park. This time of the evening it was beautiful. Busy still, but it was nice to walk along its pathways and admire the trees as they passed the zoo, and stroll under the bridges, where a trombonist was playing a version of 'Greensleeves'.

They decided to sit down on one of the benches that lined most of the paths in the park, and sat opposite an elderly couple who were feeding some biscuit crumbs to a load of birds.

'My feet are killing me.' Natalie lifted up her right foot and rolled her ankle, before doing the same with the left one.

Henry sat down beside her, his arm draped

across the back of the bench, behind her shoulders. He wasn't touching her, but she kind of liked the proprietorial nature of it.

'I guess we walk miles in our job,' she said.

'Here. Give me your feet.' Henry reached down and swung her legs around, so that he was a little further away. He now had her right foot in his hands and was removing her shoe.

'Oh, no, don't do that! My feet are probably all horrible and sweaty.' She tried to pull free.

'Your feet are lovely. Like the rest of you.'

She watched hesitantly, hardly daring to breathe, as his masterful hands expertly massaged her ankles and metacarpal bones...her toes, her lower calf muscles. She couldn't look at his face. Could only concentrate on his hands touching her, caressing her, easing out the aches and pains in her feet.

She fought the urge to groan with satisfaction as, slowly, she began to relax more and tried to enjoy it. Henry seemed to know exactly what she wanted. Exactly what her feet needed. A perk of being looked after by a medic, who knew where all the knotty little problems might be.

A smile settled upon her face and finally she looked up at him, wondering whether to tell him about the baby. He seemed so wonderful. So kind. So caring.

But I thought the same about Wade and I was wrong. Why tell him if I might lose this baby anyway?

She was still in the first trimester. Still early on. Anything could happen. Why tell him and ruin his life if it all went to hell?

'Other foot.' He lifted her left foot, dropped her shoe and began his massage again.

'You're very brave. Massaging feet that you barely know.'

He grinned. 'I'm familiar with the rest of your body. Although I think I neglected these feet the first time around.'

It was a reference to their night together. She coloured as she remembered it too, and how it had felt to have his fingers and hands exploring other places on her body.

Had it suddenly become hotter? She wanted to fan herself...

'Do you ever imagine your future?' she asked suddenly. She needed to know exactly *what* he imagined, as if it would somehow give her a clue.

'Sometimes.'

'What's in it? Marriage? Family?'

He stopped to look at her. 'What do *you* imagine?'

She looked away at the old couple, now sitting holding hands. Content with being in each other's company. Not needing to speak.

'Finding true love. Someone I can trust. Someone I could have a family with. Nice house. A dog...' She smiled, remembering their previous conversation about pets. 'What about you?'

'That all sounds perfect to me.' He smiled at her and let go of her feet, after he'd slipped her shoes back on.

She'd kind of liked having her bare feet exposed to the air, and now the shoes felt alien. Compacting. Harsh.

'And are you looking for that special someone?' she asked. 'Because back when we met you were off the market. Has that changed?'

He raised an eyebrow, smiling at her. 'What are you offering?'

What *was* she offering? She'd love to tell him that technically, his family had begun. That she was already carrying his child. But she was scared. Doing so would launch them both into the unknown. Right now he was smiling at her, and she was happy being in his company, getting to know him better. Telling him would change all that. He'd back off. He'd want time to think. And during that time she'd be left in the lurch. Again. She was done with waiting for men to make up their minds about where they wanted to be. This new life was supposed to be about her taking charge.

'I'm thinking of lots of things I could offer right now. But I'd hate to scare you.'

'I'm not that easily scared.' He smiled.

CHAPTER SIX

NATALIE WAS FEELING terrified about her twelve-week scan. What would it show? Would she hear a heartbeat? Would everything be normal?

She'd already seen her primary care physician, who'd confirmed the pregnancy, and she'd had an early scan at eight weeks, due to her medical history. Everything had been fine then. The baby was a small, curled bean. With a beating heart. But that was all. And a lot could happen in four weeks.

She was slightly reassured by her continuing symptoms. She'd always told other prospective mothers that nausea was a good sign that the pregnancy was progressing normally, although she'd never truly understood just how *bad* that nausea could be.

But the most terrifying thing about the scan was that today would be the day that she would actually see her baby. No longer a grey bean, but a foetus that would be baby-shaped. Legs.

Arms. Moving. A real person. She knew realistically that it was there, growing in her womb like a plant, but today would make it official that she was out of that first terrifying trimester. Once she *saw* that baby—its human shape, how it moved—and heard its heartbeat it would become real. And if she were to lose it after that... The heartbreak would be so much worse than she dared imagine.

She wanted this baby so much!

It was a miracle that it had survived this far. Somehow navigating its way past all her scar tissue and implanting anyway. And growing! Her body was definitely more curvaceous, and there was a tiny bump that she was managing to conceal by deliberately picking scrubs one size too large.

It had been difficult concealing the news of her pregnancy. There'd been so many times she'd wanted to tell people. Henry, obviously. And Roxy, who'd become a close friend to her since she'd started working there. Soon she would have to start telling people, and then the questions would begin from everyone.

Henry.

Her heart ached at the thought of him. How would he react? Part of her wanted him to smile and scoop her up in his arms, kiss her and tell her that everything would be fine. That he would look after her...that they would work this out. That he would be there for her and the baby and that, somehow, they would get to know each other better.

They'd been spending a lot of time together lately, out of the hospital, and each time he'd walked her home to her door and pressed a gentle kiss to her cheek, even though she craved so much more.

She had this dream that soon he would tell her everything, because he'd recognised that they were family now. That she would discover he truly was a good guy and didn't have any skeletons or ex-wives in his closet. Or current wives!

But she knew it wouldn't happen like that. Life never turned out the way she hoped. She could hardly expect him to whoop for joy at the news that his one-night stand was pregnant, no matter how much he seemed to like her.

Imagine the gossip in the hospital. Everyone would know! And he was a man who liked to keep his private life private. She didn't imagine he'd be all that impressed.

I can't worry about all that right now. I just need to get through this scan and find out if my baby is okay.

It wasn't particularly cold out, but Natalie didn't want to be recognised going into the antenatal clinic. So she put her crazy curls under a hat and wore a face mask. She figured she'd sit in a corner and keep her head down by reading a book, or something. She'd be incognito.

It felt odd, not going straight to OBGYN But she managed to get inside the hospital without anyone recognising her, and she stood in the doorway of the antenatal clinic and scanned the room first, making sure there was no one there that she knew.

Convinced she was safe, she went over to the reception desk. 'Hi, I've got a scan at one o' clock?'

'Name?' asked a receptionist she'd never met before.

'Natalie Webber,' she said in a low voice, checking around her once more.

The receptionist smiled. 'Take a seat, Ms Webber, and you'll be called through soon.'

'Thanks.'

The clinic was busy. But she knew she was one of the first on the afternoon list, and she hadn't turned up until the last possible moment, so it wasn't as if she had to sit there and wait for all these other women to be seen first.

There was a corner seat free and she went and sat down in it, over by a small playpen filled with plastic balls for younger children.

Pulling one of the books that Henry had lent her from her bag, she began to read.

She was the patient now, and that felt strange, bringing back dark thoughts of her previous time in hospital. The last time time she'd been a patient she'd had bad news delivered to her, and she hoped she wouldn't have any more now.

There were three scanning rooms. The door of the first one opened and a woman stood in the doorway, dressed in scrubs. 'Mrs Oliver?'

A woman who looked to be about five months along got up and entered the room.

Natalie looked back down at her book, but none of the words were going in.

'Miss Cortez?'

Natalie looked up again, her nerves increasing. And this time she noticed Henry, who'd come striding into Antenatal, carrying a thick folder which he passed to the lady at Reception.

Lifting her book, she held her breath. What was he doing here? He shouldn't be here! Not today of all days! She could have gone anywhere for her scan, but there'd been no appointments except at this clinic that fitted in with her shift times. She'd thought she'd be safe. Henry hardly ever came down to this department unless he was specifically called.

He was smiling and chatting easily to the

lady behind the reception desk, and Natalie could see the way the young receptionist was looking up at him. All smiles and head to one side with a tinkly laugh. Clearly flirting with him!

'Ms Webber?' called a voice.

Oh, no.

She saw Henry frown and turn to look at the roomful of women to see who would stand up. He'd clearly recognised the name.

What to do? Pretend I'm not here? No. I can't do that! I need to know my baby is all right. I have to go in there!

With trembling legs, Natalie got to her feet and tried to hurry through to the room without looking directly at Henry.

And she almost made it, too.

'Natalie?'

She stopped, heart in her mouth, stomach in knots, before turning to look at him and meeting his gaze over her mask. She pulled it beneath her chin. Gave a rueful smile.

'What are you…?'

And then realisation dawned in his eyes as guilt flooded her face, and he stood there, hands on his hips, looking down at the ground, before walking over to her and pulling her to one side.

'Are you pregnant?' he whispered urgently.

'Maybe...'

He stared at her, his face a blizzard of emotions. Anger. Shock. Surprise. Upset. Fear. Disbelief. She saw them all hit his eyes, and much, much more.

'I need to go in, Henry. They're waiting.'

'Then I'm coming in with you!'

'What? No!'

'Is this not my baby?'

She stared at him hard and swallowed, her mouth having gone incredibly dry with nerves, as she debated all the possible lies she could tell. But she knew she wouldn't say any of them, because she'd hated it when someone had told lies to her. It had ruined her world and her life.

She knew Henry had to be wondering. Wondering why she'd never mentioned her pregnancy to him in the last few weeks. Or even last night, when they'd gone to see that movie and she'd fallen asleep halfway through. He'd nudged her awake at the end and she'd made excuses about not having slept very well the night before.

'It is.'

It was as if she'd hit him with a fist the size of a house. At one point she thought he might need to sit down, he went so pale.

'Then I'm coming in. And you and I are going to talk.'

He pushed past her to enter the room where the sonographer waited.

Natalie smiled a quick greeting to the woman, who said hello, before removing her now useless mask and hat, freeing her curls, and lying down on the bed.

Henry sat on the chair beside her.

'Dr Locke! Are you Dad?' asked the sonographer with a big smile, unaware that he'd only just learned this news himself.

'I am,' he said, somewhat shakily.

Natalie glanced at him, then turned back to answer the sonographer's questions. She would deal with Henry's anger and shock later. What mattered right now was the baby.

Marissa, the sonographer, ran Natalie through a few questions. How far along was she? What was the date of her last period? What symptoms had she been experiencing? Was there any pertinent medical history she ought to know about?

'Erm…yes. I was involved in a car accident some time ago.'

'What injuries did you sustain?'

Natalie glanced at Henry, knowing that he would be hearing this for the first time. 'I broke my pelvis. My uterus was ruptured and I lost an ovary. I was told I'd probably never have children.'

'Ah, yes, I see that now. You had an earlier scan four weeks ago?'

Natalie guiltily glanced at Henry, feeling her cheeks fill with heat. 'Yes.'

'And was this a natural conception?'

'Yes.'

'Okay. Well, we'll take a look and see what we can see. The last scan was normal, and your baby was measuring at eight weeks exactly. You've been referred to Dr Yang, our specialist OBGYN, to monitor the pregnancy, considering your previous injuries?'

'Yes…' Natalie didn't want to look and see what Henry felt about these revelations. She figured he'd still be in shock about the pregnancy, never mind anything else.

'So, if you can just loosen your trousers, I'll put on some gel and get going. It can feel rather cold, okay?'

'That's fine.'

'Have you drunk plenty? Do you have a full bladder?'

'Yes.'

Self-consciously, Natalie unbuttoned her trousers, pulled down the zipper and exposed her lower abdomen to the room.

Marissa tucked some paper towel into the top of Natalie's panties to protect her clothes from the gel.

'You've already got a little bump. Look at that!'

And then she pressed the transducer against Natalie's belly.

CHAPTER SEVEN

HENRY DIDN'T KNOW what to feel—apart from completely blindsided. He'd never suspected this. Not *this*.

Pregnant.

Natalie was pregnant with his baby. And she'd known about it for some time!

A rush of emotions was threatening to overwhelm him.

When he'd found out Jenny was pregnant it had been entirely different. She'd been in her small studio, painting. He'd used to love it in there. The smell of the paints, the multicoloured paint splatters everywhere, covering every surface... Pots and jars of brushes, canvases on the walls and stacked on the floor... Her most recent commissions wrapped and ready to be shipped to their new homes.

Jenny's style could only be described as vibrant. She loved colour and used splashes of it to emphasise a figure. Nature and animals were her forte. So, for example, if she was painting an elephant the animal itself would be grey, and painted in detail, yet behind the elephant would be an expressive multitude of colours. Pinks, reds, greens, oranges, blues, yellows…

Her work had become more popular after one small piece had been bought by a minor celebrity, who had shared the work online, and suddenly Jenny's website and email inbox had become much busier with requests.

Usually whenever he'd gone in to see her working she'd been frantically at it, brush clamped between her teeth as she concentrated on some tiny detail like an eye. So that day, when he'd gone into her studio and seen her just standing there, staring at a canvas, without her usual frantic movements, he'd smiled and asked her if everything was all right.

'Uh-huh,' she'd said, still staring at the canvas he couldn't see.

'Are you stuck?'

He'd gone to stand by her, turned to look at the canvas. His eyes had opened in surprise. Because she'd not painted a rhino, or a raccoon, or a giraffe, but instead a baby, curled up tight inside a womb.

Puzzled, he'd asked her, 'Is that a new commission?'

'No,' she'd said, turning to face him. 'It's ours.'

Henry had frowned. Theirs? It wasn't typical of her usual work, and he'd had no idea where they would put it, but...

'It's nice. It's different...'

'No, Henry!' Jenny had reached for his hand then, placed it against her belly and said again, 'It's *ours*.'

It had taken a second or two for him to realise what she was actually telling him. But when it had sunk in he'd been so happy! Whirling her around the room, whooping and yelling with happiness, not caring one iota that he was probably getting paint all over his suit.

'We're having a baby!'

He'd been so happy. *They'd* been so happy. Unaware of the tragedy that was awaiting them. And now it could happen all over again. He could lose everything.

It was as if he could barely breathe. He was afraid to inhale too deeply, in case he somehow unbalanced what was happening and caused everything to crash. These next moments were fragile. What he was about to see could ruin him all over again, and he wasn't sure he was strong enough to survive another disaster of the heart.

He'd done a double-take out in Reception.

He'd brought down a file that they'd received from a primary care physician, ready for a patient they were hoping to scan later that day, and though his brain had registered the name 'Ms Webber' being called, he hadn't for one moment thought it would be Natalie.

He'd seen movement, glanced up just to check that it wasn't by some crazy coincidence *her*, and he'd seen the curls, tucked inside a hat. He had recognised her in an instant, even though she'd been trying to hide behind a face mask, and in that moment, when her eyes had locked with his, his brain had simply been unable to compute why she was there.

Because it had to be a mistake, right?

Some cosmic joke?

He'd know if she was pregnant. They'd spent so much time together lately. He'd even seen her last night! She would have said something, surely? Though, to be fair, she had been asleep for most of it…

Oh. Now it all makes sense!

The weird symptoms that she'd passed off as exhaustion from work. Looking pale. Sneaking snacks. The tears that seemingly flowed so easily every time she helped a mother give birth. Before, she'd smile and look happy for them, but…

But, no. It was real. And she'd stood there in

front of him, like a remorseful child in front of a headmaster, and told him that, yes, she was pregnant—with his baby.

And now he sat in an ultrasound room as a father. *Again.*

He still couldn't wrap his head around that word. Because the last time he'd hoped to be a father it had all gone terribly wrong. Who was to say that it would go right this time? Especially since Natalie had just revealed the exact nature of the injuries from her accident...

He decided to concentrate on the face of Marissa, the sonographer. She had the screen turned away from them, as was the usual practice, until she could turn it to show the happy parents that everything was all right. He stared intently at her face. Waiting for the inevitable frown. Waiting for the solemn information that this pregnancy wasn't viable.

'Any history of multiples in either family?' Marissa asked suddenly.

Multiples?

'No. Not in mine,' said Henry, shocked.

'My cousin has twins,' said Natalie.

Marissa smiled. 'Well, they didn't pick up on it in the first scan, but...so do you.'

She turned the screen and there, exactly as she'd just told them, were two babies. One behind the other.

'Separate sacs, so non-identical. That's carried down from the mom, so you probably released two eggs from that remaining ovary.'

Two babies.

Two eggs.

Non-identical twins.

Twins.

Henry wasn't sure if he was even breathing. He stared at the screen in absolute shock, then turned to look at Natalie and saw that she looked just as shocked as he!

'That's why I've got a bump already? That's why I've been so sick?'

Of course! Henry recalled now the multitude of times over the last few weeks when Natalie had hurriedly excused herself from a room. He'd thought on occasion that maybe she was running away from him. He'd been beginning to get a complex about it! Especially when at other times they'd seemed to be getting on so well.

It had been morning sickness?

How did I not realise? I'm a bloody OBGYN, for crying out loud!

With hindsight, it was obvious.

But...twins. Twins!

'Are they...all right?' Henry managed to ask, even though he could see quite clearly from his spot by the bed that they looked good to him.

'Looking good!' said Marissa perkily. 'I'll just get some measurements, and then we can listen to the heartbeats, if you'd like?'

Henry looked down at Natalie. Saw her lying there, vulnerable...afraid. He realised all she had been through these last few weeks. Why hadn't she told him? Why had she kept this news to herself? Because of the accident she'd mentioned? Maybe she'd thought she'd never make it to today? Maybe she was just as stunned as he to see that this pregnancy was viable?

He watched as Marissa checked the Nuchal folds, femur lengths and amniotic sacs. 'They're measuring a good size. Twelve weeks and two days for Baby A and twelve weeks and three days for Baby B.'

Baby A. Baby B.

Henry had used those terms many times before with his patients, but he'd never understood before the sheer impact of those words. He wasn't just going to be a father to one child, but to *two*.

Suddenly the small room was filled with the sound of first one heartbeat then another. Fast. Like runaway trains. It choked him up a little. He could feel a lump in his throat and was glad that at this moment he wasn't expected to speak. Because right now he doubted he'd be able to say anything.

He stared at the babies on the screen.

They were his.

He was going to be a father.

Natalie was glad to be lying down. *Twins!*

'I never suspected… Even for a moment… I've barely been able to hold on to the thought of one baby, never mind two.'

And Henry had discovered it with her.

'How was this missed before?' she asked.

'I can't say,' said Marissa. 'Maybe one of the babies was much smaller at the time. Baby B is still positioned right behind Baby A.'

This was a pivotal moment. She had nothing to hide from him anymore. It had become difficult these last few weeks, coping with the morning sickness that seemed to last all day, lying to her friends and telling them that she was all right, even though she knew they'd noted how many times she'd come into work looking off-colour. Blaming it all on tiredness.

Now she could tell them all. Because Henry knew.

It was a huge stress off her shoulders.

Having to keep a secret was the worst thing in the world!

No, this wasn't how she'd expected Henry

to find out, but he had, and it was done, and quite frankly she could already feel some of the weight being lifted.

All she had to do now was get these two babies safely through six more months.

No. Five more months. Twins come early.

Less than half a year to get her life sorted. To find a new apartment. To buy all that they'd need. How was she going to do that? One baby was expensive enough…

Marissa gave them a few copies of the ultrasound pictures and Natalie sat up and wiped the gel from her belly with blue paper towel.

'I'm going to check you've got a follow-up appointment soon with Dr Yang,' Marissa told her.

Natalie nodded. 'Well, we work with him. I'm sure we can chat to him about it.'

'Of course. He's a specialist in multiples and, considering your history, I think you've picked a most excellent doctor to see you through this.'

They both thanked her and left the room, going back out into the bright lights of the antenatal clinic's reception area.

Natalie carried her coat and her mask in her hands as they went out into the main hospital corridor. She turned to face Henry and smiled nervously. 'Surprise…'

Henry still looked in shock, but he gave a brief laugh. 'It certainly is. How are you feeling?'

'Nauseated, and… I don't know. I wasn't expecting twins. I wasn't expecting to see anything really, with my history.'

'About that… Can you tell me what happened?'

Natalie glanced at her watch. She had thirty minutes before the start of her shift. 'Aren't you working?'

'I have time for this.'

She nodded and took him over to a couple of chairs in the corridor, where they sat down.

'I knew this guy. Wade was his name. And… I thought we were in love. Well, I was in love with him. Utterly. We seemed such a great match. He was handsome and charming. He made me laugh. Most weekends we'd go out for a drive somewhere…see the sights. This one time we were driving, and somehow Wade lost control of the car. The sun got in his eyes, or something, and the next thing I knew we were careering into the next lane. We hit a truck and the car flipped. Witnesses say we rolled three times and came to land on the roof. I was knocked out, thankfully, so I didn't experience any pain until afterwards. I was rushed

to hospital with three fractures of my pelvis…
damage to my fallopian tubes and my womb.
They removed an ovary, but managed to save
my uterus. I was told the likelihood of my getting pregnant without assistance would be a
miracle. Guess they were wrong about that!'
She gave a bitter laugh.

'And Wade? What happened to him?' asked
Henry.

Natalie shook her head and grimaced. 'His
wife arrived.'

She watched as Henry took this in.

He looked down at the ground. 'I'm sorry.'

'I couldn't believe it. I kept waiting for him
to come to my bedside. To apologise. To say
that they were splitting up, or something. I kept
texting him. Asking him to come and see me.
Only he didn't. But *she* did. Her name was Bea.
She stood at the end of my bed and told me she
was sorry I'd been hurt, but she'd been hurt
more, and that Wade was a serial adulterer. She
said that if I still wanted him I could have him,
as she was walking away.'

Natalie shook her head.

'I'd just been told I wouldn't ever get pregnant without a lot of medical help. I felt I'd
lost my ability to have children. I hoped that I
wouldn't lose him too, at first. It all seemed too

much. But then I got angry as more and more time passed. Obviously I didn't take her up on her offer. He had kids. Two boys. Six and nine years of age. How didn't I know? How didn't I see?'

'The same way I didn't know that you were pregnant. Why didn't you tell me? You must have known for weeks!'

Natalie looked down at the ground. 'I'm sorry. I just…' She ran out of words and shrugged.

'You and I have got a lot to sort out.'

'I guess we do.'

'I'll speak to Dr Yang. Go over your medical files—if you'll allow me to?'

'Okay.'

'And we'll take the rest of this one day at a time?'

She nodded. 'I guess.'

They stood looking at one another awkwardly.

'Henry?'

'Yes?'

'I need you to be honest with me. I can't be lied to again. It's too much. So, tell me this, at least. I know I've been to your apartment, and it didn't look like you had someone living with you, but… Are you married? Do you have a wife or a girlfriend I need to worry about?'

He stared intently into her eyes. 'No. I used to be married, at home in England, but we got divorced. That's all over now.'

She stared back at him, seeing the truth in his eyes. Believing him. 'Okay. All right. Then one day at a time it is.'

'One day at a time.'

He took her hand in his and gave it a reassuring squeeze.

Finding an empty delivery room, Henry closed the door behind him and walked over to the window, rubbing his hands through his hair, unable to actually believe what just happened.

The day had begun so innocently. So *normally.*

Now this. A father. To twins.

What if the same thing that had happened to Jenny happened to Natalie? After hearing her story about Wade—how she was lied to, deceived—he knew Natalie deserved to know the truth about his and Jenny's baby. But how could he have told her in that moment, when all she'd needed from him was reassurance that he wasn't about to bolt and leave her behind.

He couldn't have told her then. It had not been the time to stress her out unnecessarily. But he would have to find the time to do so soon.

She has to know.

But what would be the best way to let her know?

I could invite her round for dinner. We need to talk more anyway. Get to know each other properly if we're going to be parents.

If.

It could all go wrong. His track record in these matters didn't bode well. Nothing had worked out for him so far—why should he expect this pregnancy to be any different? Even though they'd found no specific reason for the stillbirth of his last child, they were up against so many unknowns with Natalie's internal injuries.

Oh, God, I'm going to lose them, too!

The thought of Natalie going through what Jenny had…

Henry sagged as he stood by the window, feeling all his fight go out of him at that moment. He'd put on a front just now. Pretended to be strong for Natalie. But he was terrified.

Turning, he left the room, going to look for her, finding her about to go into a patient's room.

'Natalie?'

He saw her turn, see him, smile. 'Hey.'

'Look, I've been thinking… We've both got a lot to unpack over the next few months and…

um… I think it would be a good idea for us to sit down over dinner. At my place. Discuss a few things.'

'Oh…um…sure. That sounds good, I guess…'

He smiled. 'Great. Can you do tonight? Tomorrow? The weekend?'

She laughed. 'Tonight's fine. Say, eight o'clock?'

'Perfect. What kind of things do you like to eat at the moment?'

'Anything tangy.'

'Sweet and sour chicken?'

She nodded. 'Sounds good,' she said again.

'Okay. I'll see you this evening, then.'

'You will.'

She smiled at him, making her eyes gleam, before she entered the patient's room.

Henry stood there for a moment, quite unable to believe that he was actually inviting a woman to his place for a meal. It had been a long, long time since he'd invited someone to dinner. The last woman he'd brought back to his New York apartment—in fact the only woman—had been Natalie.

And now he was inviting her again.

Because they were going to become a family.

If everything worked out right, that dream he'd always had could be about to come true.

How was he supposed to feel about that?

He had vowed to stay single, and now here he was, going to be a father to twins, inviting the mother of his children for a meal.

Boy, how the tables could turn!

Natalie peered up at the building in front of her. She'd been here once before. On New Year's Eve. Or rather, New Year's Day. In the early hours. Stumbling into the elevator. Unable to take her hands off Henry, her lips pressed to his as they struggled with clothes, desperate to get inside his place and consummate their lust for each other.

If they'd known ahead of time the results of that night, would they still have done it?

She stepped through the revolving doors and across the lobby. She didn't recognise it. But why should she? That night she'd only had eyes for Henry, and if there'd been a trio of dancing pink elephants in the lobby she probably wouldn't have noticed.

It was very stylish. Black marbled floor with hints of white and gold. A welcome desk behind which stood a suited building manager, who smiled at her approach.

'May I help you, madam?'

'I've come to see Dr Locke on Floor Ten.'

'You have his apartment number?'

'I do.' She smiled, feeling her stomach bubble with nerves as she headed towards the elevator and pressed the button.

She was still reeling from the news today. The severity of her nausea was now explained, by the news that she was carrying more than one baby! And what had once seemed like a simple new life in the big city had changed in an instant into something wholly more complicated and involved.

She'd vowed to remain single as she began this New Year, and yet here she was, into March now, pregnant with twins and about to have dinner with the father of her children.

How crazy was that?

She'd called her family. Told them. Of course they'd been full of questions! Her mom had wanted to see her. Asked if she could visit. But she'd got no room to put her mother up, so she'd promised to fly home for a weekend visit soon.

The elevator doors pinged open and she stepped aside as a woman pushing a stroller with a screaming toddler in it whooshed past.

Natalie watched her go…watched her struggle to answer her cell phone as her child protested and tried to climb out of the stroller, face all red with tears, and wondered if that was her future.

Nervous about what awaited them both, she stepped into the elevator and pressed the button for the tenth floor. She felt her stomach drop as the elevator raced upwards, and before she knew it she was on the tenth floor and walking towards Henry's apartment. There was the ghost of a memory here. Her laughing, feeling Henry's lips against her neck as he vainly searched his pocket for his keys. She'd tried to help him, hands wandering, finding an entirely more interesting bulge in his pants and focusing her attention on that instead.

Natalie felt her cheeks blush with heat, unable to believe that she'd been so brazen with him. But hadn't she been throwing caution to the wind, truly believing that it was just for one night only? That if she *acted* confident she'd *be* confident?

She raised her hand and knocked on his door. Clearing her throat and trying to look normal. She'd spent an age deciding what to wear. They'd been out together so many times already, but this seemed more official.

She heard him slide off the keychain and then the door opened and there he stood, dressed casually in dark jeans and a black tee, revealing the muscles in his arms and his narrow, flat waist. Natalie tried hard not to think too much about what lay beneath those clothes.

'Hi.' She smiled.

'Hey, come on in.'

He stepped forward to kiss her on the cheek. She closed her eyes. Paused. Revelled in the sensation of his lips once again on her skin. It was sending her pulse rate rocketing, and her temperature had soared by what felt like five degrees. Would she ever get used to it?

Natalie stepped past him and into the apartment, her eyes widening slightly as a rush of memories returned. Searching for her panties. Her bra. Finding the heels that she'd kicked off haphazardly in this very hall. Grabbing her bag and trying to be as quiet as she could as she unlocked his door and snuck away whilst he was in the shower.

Now she could focus on the things that had only been in the periphery of her attention that night. The framed paintings on the walls. A tiger set against a splash of bright colours…a hissing snake about to attack, framed by explosions of green and orange.

'Interesting art.'

Henry smiled and nodded. 'I…er…know the artist.'

'Oh?' Natalie peered closer at the painting of the snake, tried to decipher the author's signature. It looked like *J Locke*…

'My wife painted them.'

She turned to stare at him, wondering what kind of man kept his ex-wife's paintings on the wall? A man who still had a thing for her? Who hoped to re-establish their relationship?

Henry must have seen the questions in her eyes. The doubt. The fear.

'Don't worry. It's totally over. I just happen to really like these two. I had about twenty, and sold most of them, but these I bought from her before we even got married, so…'

She shook her head. 'You don't have to explain yourself to me.'

'I do, though. We're going to be parents. Hopefully.'

He smiled and led the way to his living room. A large open space that was very masculine. Lots of dark furniture. Black couches. Black cushions. White walls. Lots of green plants, either on the walls or trailing from pots up on high. There was a huge television in the centre of the room. A piano beside it. And a gaming system.

'You like to play?'

'On occasion. Can I get you a drink?'

'Do you have orange juice?'

He nodded. 'Fresh, with pulp.'

'Sounds perfect, thank you.'

He nodded and indicated a couch. 'Take a seat. I'll be back in a moment.'

Natalie slowly lowered herself onto the couch and made a soft sound at finding how wonderfully comfortable it was. She settled back, adjusting a cushion behind her, just as Henry came back with a tall glass of fresh orange juice that he sat on a coaster on the black glass coffee table in front of her. He sat opposite with his own glass.

'Hope you're hungry?' he said.

'I'm always hungry. Anything to stave off the nausea.'

'I'm sorry you've been suffering.'

'It's certainly been difficult hiding it.'

Henry looked awkward for a moment. Then curious. 'Can I ask why you didn't tell me?'

She looked up at him as she took a sip of her juice. Right to the meat of the conversation already?

'Good question.' She sighed. 'I was scared. Plain and simple. Shocked to even be pregnant in the first place. And then, because of my situation, my history, I just assumed I wouldn't make it through the first trimester. I didn't see any point in disrupting your life until I had something definite to tell you.'

'Like today?'

She nodded. 'Like today. I needed to see that scan. I thought if they told me that everything was going okay, then I would find a way to tell you. I promise.'

'You would have told me?'

'Yes. Even though I know it's not something you wanted or planned after a one-night stand. I figured you were a guy who'd want to start his family from within marriage. Out of love.'

'We don't always get what we want. Often we get what we need...'

'If I hurt you, that wasn't my intention. I was trying, in my own faulty way, to protect you from pain.'

He pondered her words solemnly, then nodded.

'I've had some time to get used to this idea and I do want them. I want them very much. These babies.' She laughed. 'Still seems strange to say that. *Babies*. Plural.'

Henry agreed. 'You're right. It sounds crazy. Unreal. If you'd have told me I don't think I would have believed it, so I'm glad I was at the scan.'

'You must have done a double-take when you realised they were calling for me.'

'I'll say.'

Natalie laughed. 'I'm sorry, Henry. That you discovered it in that way. I would have wanted to tell you in a nicer way. Maybe sat you down for a coffee in the hospital cafeteria...broken the news...surreptitiously slipped the scan pictures across the table to you...'

He smiled. 'Life likes to play with people, that's for sure.'

She thought back to the crash. To seeing Wade's wife walk into her room. 'It does.'

They were both silent for a minute, and then Henry got to his feet. 'I'd better start cooking. You must be starving, and it's been a big day for both of us.'

'Can I help you?' she asked.

'If you'd like.'

She followed him into the kitchen. Saw that it was an extension of the living area. All sleek black surfaces. The only colour in the kitchen came from the large bowl of fruit on the centre island.

'Here. You measure out and rinse the rice and I'll chop up the chicken.'

It was nice cooking with Henry. He was at ease in the kitchen and clearly cooked a lot for himself. He whizzed from cupboard to drawer, selecting implements and pots and pans. His skill with a knife was undeniable, and he had the chicken cut up within seconds, before sliding the meat into the hot wok he was using to cook with.

The meat hissed and began to sizzle as Natalie chopped peppers and onions. The onions were strong and began to make her eyes water.

Henry noticed and grabbed a piece of paper

towel. He stood in front of her, dabbing at her eyes. 'Okay?'

She nodded. 'Thanks.'

He did little things like that, she'd noticed. Like in the park, when she'd mentioned her feet hurt and he'd massaged them. Like when he'd brought all the midwives drinks because they hadn't got away for a break or a drink all day. Other things, too. Little things. Smiling at her over his mask in the OR. Raising an eyebrow as if to ask if she was okay. Sharing a joke with her that he thought she'd like. Bringing her books he thought she might enjoy.

She'd got so used to not being noticed that to finally be *seen* was just...nice. Odd. But strangely comforting.

She studied Henry's face carefully as he concentrated hard on gently mopping away her onion tears. He was an extremely handsome man. Brilliant blue eyes, dark hair, a square, dashing jaw peppered by stubble at this time of the evening. And he was being so gentle with her!

For a brief moment their eyes met. And being that close...staring into each other's eyes... became incredibly intimate. And uncomfortable.

Natalie had to laugh and turn away, desperate for more but afraid to let it happen. They'd already had so much news today—did they really want to add a new frisson to their relationship?

Soon the rice was gently simmering away, and the kitchen was filled with enough delicious smells to make her stomach begin to rumble. She watched Henry as he stirred the chicken and vegetables together in the sauce, reduced the heat. She saw the muscles flex in his arm, felt her gaze drop to his beautiful backside in those dark jeans, and felt another stirring far below her midriff.

'Tell me about your wife. What kind of woman was she?'

Natalie needed to know. Needed to know what kind of woman had snagged this man into marriage. What kind of woman had made this man think, *Yes, she is the one I want to be married to for the rest of my life.*

Henry thought for a moment. 'Her name is Jenny. She's English—like me. She was an art student when we met, madly into painting—as you've already seen. And she was the complete opposite of me.'

'Opposites attract?' Natalie smiled.

'I guess... I like neatness and order. Jenny likes anarchy. Disorder. Disarray. I was the one who put away clothes. Jenny didn't care if they hung off the backs of chairs, or stayed on the floor because she'd missed when she'd thrown them into the laundry basket.'

She could hear the admiration that Henry still had for his ex-wife in his voice. Did he love her still?

The thought made her anxious, even though she knew she had no claim on this man romantically. They might have made two babies, but that did not mean they would have a relationship going forward. They hadn't established what they were. Or what type of claim they had on each other.

'We had a whirlwind relationship,' he went on. 'Too fast, probably. But Jenny was manic—she actually got diagnosed with bipolar just after we got married—and rushing into a relationship seemed to make sense to her. It was how she was. It was how she did things. In a rush. Chaotic. Just reacting.'

'Was it bad? Did she have to take medication?'

Henry drained the rice and began to serve it onto two plates. 'Yes, she did. Sometimes she'd forget to take it, but mostly she remembered.'

Natalie wondered what had broken them up? Had it been the bipolar? 'What happened between you two?'

Henry passed her a plate after adding some of the sweet and sour chicken, and indicated that they should go through to the living area, where there was a table and chairs for them so they could sit down and eat. He didn't speak until they were seated, but she could see he looked extremely uncomfortable.

'I find it hard to talk about the next phase of my life. I've not spoken about it with anybody from work. No one knows.'

He was asking for her discretion. She got that. And if she wanted to know about this man she had to give it. She made a zipping motion across her lips and smiled.

'Jenny fell pregnant.'

Natalie stared. This was what she had dreaded. She knew he'd been married, knew there was an ex-wife out there—but children, too? Her simple, ordinary life was becoming more and more complicated by the minute, and now she'd learned that her own children, if they made it through the pregnancy, would have a half-sibling. She would become part of a blended family, with all the baggage that entailed.

'Oh.' She pushed the food around on her plate. Despite her hunger, she found she didn't really want to eat, but the nausea kept insisting.

Eat, or I'll make you regret it!

'We'd not planned it, and when she found out she stopped taking her bipolar medication, because there'd been a report about some risks during the first trimester.'

Natalie said nothing, just continued to listen.

'Her bipolar symptoms returned, but she refused to go back on the tablets and instead turned to her painting. Mostly she was manic. On a high. Working furiously in her studio, creating painting after painting. Never stopping. Never resting. Working all through the night. There were occasional lows, during which she'd sleep for almost an entire day. And because of the highs and lows we didn't pay as much attention to her pregnancy as we could have, and didn't notice when towards the end of the pregnancy the baby's movements were slowing.'

Natalie locked eyes with Henry, suddenly dreading what was to come.

'The baby...a girl...died in utero.'

Henry took a moment to gather himself as he moved to the window of his tenth-floor apartment and looked out across the city.

Natalie's heart broke for him. What he and Jenny must have gone through! That was awful... She'd helped mothers give birth to stillborn babies and knew it was one of the most heart-wrenching things any midwife had to do. They had to remain stoic and detached as much as they could, to protect themselves, but also show that they were human and grieving along with the family, maybe shedding a tear or two in private. It was a hard enough situation for the midwife. God only knew how awful it must feel to be the parents who went through that terrible trauma.

'Jenny...she...er...went downhill afterwards. We thought it was postnatal depression, but the bipolar complicated matters. We couldn't get her stable on her meds and she began to suffer hallucinations. And then she tried to kill herself.' Henry looked at Natalie. 'I got her into a private treatment facility for her own safety. To help her deal with her grief and bipolar issues. She refused to see me.'

'Why?'

'She blamed me. Said her life had been fine until she met me and that everything had gone wrong as soon as we got married. So you see... that's why I haven't let myself get close to anyone since then.'

'What happened wasn't your fault.'

'But she was right. Her life *was* fine until she met me. I'm a doctor. I should have been on top of things. Found her meds that would keep her stable. Supported her better after the stillbirth delivery. But I was grieving myself. I tried my best. I really did. But I failed.'

Natalie felt fear assail her. What had been the cause of their baby being stillborn? What if it was somehow genetic and the damage had been passed onto their twins? She already had a difficult enough path in front of her, because of her injuries from the car accident. What if another danger had been added, now, too?

'I can see it in your eyes,' said Henry. 'You're wondering if our babies will be affected, too. But I have no idea if they're at risk. There were no significant findings that explained the still-birth.'

'I think I'm allowed to be scared, Henry, after you telling me this.'

'I know. And this is why I don't get close to anyone.'

She tried not to show how much it hurt that he'd retreated from her as he stepped away from the window and began to pace the room.

'Don't get me wrong, Natalie. I'm going to be there for you and the babies. I'll support you through everything, and somehow we'll work this out. I just don't know how yet.'

Work this out? He made it sound as if she was some sort of business problem that he was managing. Were they just words? Was Henry trying to keep an emotional distance from her?

'Okay… Well, we'll just have to take it one day at a time. Like we said before. And I'll be vigilant. But I can't feel them moving yet. It's still too early.'

'You'll feel it earlier with twins—you know that.'

'I do. And I'll keep you informed.'

If he was going to sound businesslike, then so would she—even if inside she felt incredibly disappointed that she didn't seem to be getting any closer to him. She was carrying his babies! She was going to be the mother of his children!

I'll give him as much reassurance as he needs.

Henry escorted her home. It was dark, and he didn't like the idea of her travelling home alone in the big city. Especially not now.

He walked her right up to her door, waited for her to find her keys, and when she turned to say goodbye, with a smile, he leant in to kiss her on the cheek—as he always had before.

He wasn't sure if he should, because now their relationship had changed. In fact, he hesitated…looked into her eyes to see if his peck on the cheek would be welcome. But she smiled, shyly so he kissed her, inhaling the soft scent of her skin, feeling his senses overwhelmed with need and want, before he stepped back and watched her go inside.

She gave him a small smile before she closed the door, and afterwards he turned to go home.

He felt relief that he'd finally told her about Jenny, and what had happened to their daughter, and he was grateful to finally feel some of that burden lifted by sharing it with someone. But Natalie was probably the worst person he could ever have shared that with, simply because of the situation they found themselves in.

Had he terrified her with his past? Would she honour her words about keeping him informed about the babies? Or would she run for the hills, back to the safety and security of her family? She had no one in this city apart from her work colleagues and him—and what was he to her, really? A one-night stand that had evolved into a complicated friendship.

Today had been dazzling in its confusion. To find out he was going to become a father. To twins. Then to learn of Natalie's internal injuries, which could threaten the pregnancy. Telling her of his own difficult past.

He wanted to be able to celebrate the fact that he was going to be a father—wanted to love these babies. But he refused to let himself.

He could not allow himself to have hope.

Or to want. Or wish.

He had to remain at a distance until these babies were safely delivered, but it would be, oh, so difficult because of his growing feelings for Natalie.

They'd been complicated before, but now... Knowing that she was growing his children within her... He wanted to wrap his arms around her, hold her close and keep her safe. He wanted to kiss her and never let her go. Let her know that she was his and that he would be there to protect her for as long as she needed.

But was he being crazy? He'd failed Jenny—ruined his wife's life. Could he really take the chance on not ruining another?

Natalie had accepted his kiss goodbye, but did she think that was all it was? Was he being a total idiot for assuming that she would somehow read something more into it? As if he was some sort of prize catch for any woman?

Because he didn't feel that way. Not at all. He felt as if he might ruin Natalie's life if he wasn't careful. What he needed to do—what would be safest for him to do—was take a step back until these babies were born and in that immediate postnatal period. Then, and only then, would he allow himself to truly love them. Then, and only then, would he allow himself to care about Natalie.

But who am I kidding? I already care for her. I can feel it! I'm fighting it every day! But I'll just have to hide it.

* * *

Natalie had been assigned the patient with uterine didelphys—two uteruses—as apparently she had gone into early labour.

Dr Yang had prescribed tocolytics to try and prevent or slow the contractions overnight, but nothing seemed to be working, and Claudia Bateman was now in fully established labour.

'Monitor her closely, Nurse Webber,' Dr Yang had instructed, asking her to contact him the second she got to ten centimetres or the baby showed any signs of distress.

In the meantime, Henry kept popping into the room to check on this special patient, too.

'Hi, how's everything going, Claudia? Nervous?'

'Yes. It's too early! She's only thirty weeks.'

'We're keeping a very close eye on you and the baby. Natalie here is one of our best midwives.'

He smiled at Natalie and she smiled back, thankful for his faith in her abilities and his compliment. She'd had a difficult night last night, after Henry had dropped her off at home. Her mind had been whirring with thoughts, her emotions and fears pulling her this way and that. She'd not known what to think!

On the one hand she wanted to be cautious about this pregnancy, but after seeing the two babies on the scan yesterday…hearing their heartbeats… It was hard not to be optimistic and start daydreaming about the kind of life she was going to have. The kind of mother she was going to be.

She'd hated Henry walking away, leaving her at her door, knowing he was going home to his place whilst she stayed at hers. She'd started wondering about what kind of family they'd be. Was it just going to be her and the twins? Would she be a single mother, with Henry taking them at weekends? There was definitely something between them. Physically they were attracted to one another, and emotionally she wanted to be close to him—to feel that maybe they could become a family. He had escorted her home and kissed her on the cheek, as usual. But there'd been something in his eyes last night…an expression she couldn't define.

Henry had promised to be there for them. To support them. But what did that mean?

Financially? Physically? Emotionally?

Natalie wanted to dream of having it all! The cute babies and the hot guy who adored her and loved her. The white picket fence around a beautiful home in the suburbs. The two of them raising their babies with love and affection and laughter.

Who wouldn't want that?

But she sensed Henry's uncertainty. He'd told her outright—*'We'll work this out. I just don't know how yet.'* And she'd felt it in the distance he'd kept from her as he'd walked her home. Always at least two feet away, hands in pockets, when she'd yearned for him to walk with his arm around her shoulders. She'd felt it in that kiss goodbye. On her cheek. A kiss that *friends* might give one another.

She'd gone to his place last night hoping to cement their new relationship, but it was just as uncertain as it had always been.

She understood his uncertainty. Of course she did! She had it herself. But…couldn't he make a leap of faith? Couldn't he show her that she meant something to him? That she was worth something? More than just the physical carrier of his children?

Natalie was in a situation in which she needed certainty. Not vague promises. And Henry wasn't giving her pie-in-the-sky promises—he was telling her the truth. Outright. That he didn't know how they were going to do this.

Was it enough? Enough for a woman who'd just found out she was carrying twins?

Natalie dragged her attention back to Claudia, who was trying to breathe through her contractions. When her latest one was over, Natalie began asking her questions.

'Did you always know of your unique situation?'

Claudia shook her head. 'No. I only found out when I went for my first pregnancy scan.'

'It must have been a shock?' said Natalie, understanding how such a revelation could rock your world.

'That's an understatement! To find out you're some kind of medical anomaly… It makes you very popular all of a sudden.' Claudia smiled ruefully.

'One for the textbooks?' asked Henry.

'For sure!' She crunched through an ice chip. 'It's like the doctors forget…no offence intended—' she glanced at Henry '—that beneath the anomaly you're also a human being. With feelings. With worries. All they see is how different you are. How they can write a paper on you and get it published.'

'Like you're being used?' Natalie mused.

'Exactly! Yes, I'm different—but I'm also just the same as every other woman in this place. I'm going to have a baby for the first time and I'm terrified. That's what should be important. Dr Yang was the first doctor who saw me for who I am. Not *what* I am.'

Natalie wondered what Henry saw her as. As

a woman terrified to have not just one, but two babies? As a first-time mother, who was petrified because of her past injuries? As a woman who had the same fears as every other mother? Getting through the pregnancy, giving birth to healthy babies and becoming a mother to them... Or did he just see her as a problem to overcome? Something to work out? He was a very private individual. What would happen when everyone heard that they were going to have twins together? The gossip was going to be unstoppable in a place such as this.

'Well, thankfully you have someone who loves and supports you. That must mean everything when you feel the world is against you. Where *is* Alex?'

Alex was Claudia's husband.

'He left the camera in the car. He's just gone to fetch it.'

Henry was keeping an eye on the trace, tracking back through the last few contractions.

'Everything looking good there, Doc?' Claudia asked.

'Absolutely.' Henry smiled. 'Natalie, can you get me a set of obs, please?'

'Sure.'

She busied herself checking Claudia over. Everything was looking good. Her pressure was stable, her temperature was perfect...

Natalie bent over to pick up the pen she'd just dropped, and when she stood she felt the room reel a little as a wave of nausea overcame her.

She must have made a noise. Perhaps groaned a little. Because suddenly Henry was at her side.

'What is it? Are you all right?' he whispered, low and urgent.

'Yeah, I'm just feeling a little…' She rubbed at her stomach, knowing she needed to get something to eat.

'Go. Take a break,' he insisted.

'I'm fine.'

'No. You're not. You need to look after yourself.'

'Is everything okay?' Claudia asked. 'You're whispering. It's not nice when you're labouring and people whisper.'

Natalie was about to protest that everything was fine, but Henry got there first.

'Nurse Webber's fine. Just pregnant. I'm telling her she needs to eat.'

Natalie felt her cheeks flame with heat. *He was telling a patient!*

'Oh, congratulations!' Claudia said, reaching for another ice chip. 'How far along are you?'

'Just three months,' she muttered, not sure if it was tempting fate to talk about the twins so openly to anyone.

'You'll feel better soon, then, but that morning sickness is a killer, isn't it?'

Henry turned to Natalie. 'Go on. I'll come and check on you in a minute.'

'I'll be back shortly,' she said to her patient, glaring at Henry before leaving the room and heading for her locker, where a bevy of biscuits awaited.

In the staff room, armed with ginger biscuits and a banana, she sat on one of the couches, her feet up on the table. That had been a close one! Those waves of nausea could just hit her out of nowhere. But she would never complain about it. It was a good sign and it meant that the babies were still doing well.

A few moments later Roxy came into the staff room, saw Natalie with her feet up and laughed. 'Like that already, is it?'

Natalie smiled. 'You know how it is…'

'You're telling me. Mind you, you do look a little peaky. Everything okay?'

At that moment Henry came in. He sat beside Natalie and looked her over. 'Do you want to tell her?'

Natalie glared at Henry again. Did he want to tell the whole world?

'Ooh! Tell me what?' asked Roxy, settling down beside them both.

'I'm…er…pregnant,' Natalie said, feeling

terribly awkward and embarrassed. She wasn't ready to tell people yet. The more people she told, the more real it made the babies and the more she grew attached. And if something went wrong...

'You are?' Roxy's eyes widened and she gasped out loud. 'Oh, my God! Congratulations!' She threw her arms around Natalie and gave her a squeeze. 'I guess I should have known. You have looked quite green for a while, always rushing off to the bathroom, but you know how it is...you don't like to suggest something like this, because if it isn't true... How far along are you?'

'Three months.'

'Really? Oh, you should be feeling better soon, then. Unless it's twins!' Roxy laughed again, then stopped when she saw Natalie and Henry passing looks between them. 'It's *twins*?'

Natalie nodded, then smiled, unable to stop herself being caught up in Roxy's awe and wonderment as she squealed her delight.

'Who's the father? You've never mentioned a boyfriend.'

Natalie glanced at Henry again, not wanting to tell his secret unless he was the one wishing it to be known.

'I am.' Henry turned to face Roxy and smiled.

'You're kidding me?' Roxy looked from one to the other. 'Really? How? When?'

'We met at New Year's…' Natalie admitted.

'You did? Oh, my God, I can't believe it!' Roxy shook her head. 'And so you two—you're an item?'

Natalie didn't know how to answer that.

'We're working it out,' Henry said diplomatically.

'Who's in with Claudia?' Natalie asked, suddenly changing the subject, not wanting the conversation to carry on in a direction in which she didn't want to hear the answers.

'Dr Yang and her husband, Alex.'

She nodded. 'Rox, could you give us a minute?'

'Sure! Absolutely! Must give the lovebirds their moment alone!' She grinned wildly, grabbed a chocolate or two from a tin on the table and sauntered out through the door.

Natalie looked at Henry. 'So we're suddenly telling people now?'

'You're beginning to show.'

She straightened her uniform over her bump. It was more noticeable in this than in scrubs. 'You do realise that everyone will know by the end of the day now?'

He nodded. 'I don't care.'

'You don't?'

'No. You're what's important.'

'I am?'

'Of course you are,' he insisted.

How important am I to you, Henry? she wanted to ask him.

But she was too scared of hearing the answer in case it was the wrong one. *Because you're carrying my children.*

When all she wanted to hear from him… from anyone…was, *Because you mean the world to me. And I would lay my life down on the ground before you if it would keep you safe.*

But no one had ever said that to her. Or treated her in that way.

And she doubted Henry would say it, either.

She wanted him to take her face in his hands and bring her lips to his. She wanted him to settle beside her on the couch and wrap himself around her and hold her close, whispering sweet nothings into her ear and making her laugh and smile.

What the hell is going on with me?

'How are you feeling now? Stomach better?' he asked.

She nodded, slightly mollified by the soft, caring tone in his voice. 'I ought to get back to Claudia.'

'Take your time. I don't need you passing out during her delivery.'

Henry stood up and turned to go.

'Henry?'

He stopped. Looked at her. 'Yes?'

'I…' She couldn't think what to say! She needed some reassurance, that was all. Needed some sign from him that this was all going to turn out well. But those words and questions got stuck in her throat, so she copped out with another question. 'Have you spoken to Dr Yang yet about me?'

'No. Not yet. I was going to sit down with him later on today.'

'All right,' she answered quietly, and watched him disappear through the door.

Frustrated, she threw her banana skin onto the low table, angry with herself. Why couldn't she just ask him outright for what she wanted? Why didn't she demand to be treated better? With more consideration? With more…what?

Emotion? Feelings? Commitment?

How can I demand that of him? Knowing what he has already gone through?

Her stomach had settled now. She picked up the banana skin and dumped it in the bin. Took a drink of water and then headed back to Claudia.

CHAPTER EIGHT

CLAUDIA'S BABY WAS born three hours later, emerging into the world with an attempt at a roar, before she was rushed off to the NICU for monitoring and help with her breathing.

Natalie was clearing up the room, clandestinely watching Claudia being cared for and comforted by her husband, Alex. He was being the perfect partner. Holding her hand tightly. Telling his wife how much he loved her. How proud he was of her. How their daughter was beautiful and just like her momma. Asking her if there was anything she needed.

She wished a man would look at her in that way. Wished Henry would. Sometimes she thought that he did, but then convinced herself she was just imagining things.

It was strange. Confusing. Hoping for something that just a few months ago she'd been trying to stay away from.

How quickly our lives change.

'I need to see my daughter,' Claudia cried, dabbing at her eyes with a tissue. 'I haven't even held her! She needs to know her mom loves her.'

'I can take you,' Natalie offered.

Claudia sniffed, looking over at her with hope. 'You can?'

'Sure. I can grab a wheelchair and take you up now. Give me a moment to call NICU to let them know, and then I'll grab you a chair.'

Claudia beamed. 'Thank you!'

'No problem.' Natalie smiled back, glad she could help.

Once the room was cleared, she headed off to the desk to dial the NICU and tell them they'd be receiving a visitor. Then she grabbed a wheelchair and whisked Claudia and her husband off to the elevator, as the NICU was on the next floor up.

As they headed out onto the NICU floor Natalie saw Henry and Dr Yang talking to one of the neonatal specialists. She saw Henry glance up, do a double-take, and then he was striding over to her, taking her arm and pulling her politely off to one side.

'What are you doing?' he demanded.

'Claudia wants to visit her daughter.'

'Please tell me Alex pushed the wheelchair?'

Natalie frowned. 'No. I did.'

'Are you crazy?'

'I beg your pardon?' she asked incredulously.

'Natalie...you shouldn't be pushing patients around in wheelchairs. Not in your fragile condition.'

'Who are you calling fragile?'

He sighed. 'You're not. Obviously you're not. But the babies could be. They've already got enough difficulties without you hauling patients around.'

'I see. This is your cack-handed way of trying to keep me safe. Is that right?'

Henry tilted his head this way, then that, as he considered her question. Then he smiled, sighed, and said, 'Possibly. I'm sorry.'

'No, it's good. It's just... I have to be able to do my job, Henry.'

'I know. Just...don't take any unnecessary risks, okay?'

'Okay. So, do you want to push Claudia over to see her daughter, then?'

He nodded. 'Fine.'

They both went back to Claudia.

'Your daughter is over here in this bay,' Henry told her. 'She's doing well. Please don't be concerned by all the wires and cables. They're there to monitor her heart rate, temperature, blood pressure...and that one there on her face is giving her supplemental oxygen.'

Henry parked Claudia up and put the brake on the wheelchair. Claudia stood up to peer inside her daughter's warmer. Her husband, Alex, went to the other side to peer down at her.

'She's beautiful!'

Natalie stared at them, wondering if she would have this moment in a few months' time. But she would have two cribs to visit. Would her babies make it to nine months? Or would the scarring on her womb prevent it from expanding to its full size? Would her scars rupture? Would she have to deliver her twins as an emergency? She'd seen enough parents sitting by their babies' empty cribs to know that she did not want to have that in her future.

Her heart ached in that moment.

'I've spoken to Dr Yang,' Henry said in a low voice as he came to stand beside her.

'What did he say?'

'That he wants to do a detailed ultrasound himself.'

'Did he sound worried? Did he say I was high risk?'

'No. He said it's a complication, but that if we monitor the babies regularly, then we should be okay.'

'What does he mean by "regularly"?'

'Every two weeks.'

Natalie nodded. It would give them all peace

of mind to do that, so if any problems began to present themselves they could be right on it. 'Did you tell him about what happened with Jenny, too?'

Henry nodded, looking glum. 'I think I surprised him.'

'I'm sure you did. Listen, do you fancy grabbing something to eat together at lunch? About one? In the main cafeteria?'

'We should—with the gossip mill firing on all cylinders.'

'Okay. I'd better get back. Can you get a porter to bring Claudia down?'

'I will.'

Natalie smiled at him and walked away, but the second her face could not be seen by him she frowned. Was Henry's main focus the babies? It was hers, too, but she really would like a sign that he felt something for *her* as well. She herself was finding it difficult to work out how she felt, but she did at least acknowledge she had feelings for Henry.

Of course she did! How could she not? He was hot. Her hormones were raging and she was carrying his children! They were going to be a family and she wanted to spend more time with him. Hence the suggestion of lunch. They still had a lot to sort out, but she wasn't trying to drag him into a relationship he didn't want.

Even if I want one.

They'd been getting along so well together. The time she'd spent with him had told her that he really was a good guy. Maybe one of the best. And she truly trusted that he had no further secrets lurking in his past.

She knew about his past now. Knew his secrets. There was no current wife or girlfriend hiding in the wings. Henry wasn't using her. He was free and single, so she felt she could trust him in that regard. But...did he feel anything for *her* at all? Beyond friendship?

She needed to know. Because if she knew he didn't think of her in that way then she could stop hoping. She could get on with her life and put these babies to the forefront. Be the best mother she could be.

But if he *did* feel something for her...

Well, that would be a different story, wouldn't it?

If he had feelings for her they could build on that—and maybe, just maybe, she could get her happily-ever-after?

Henry spotted Natalie sitting over by a window. She already had food and drink in front of her, so he gave her a quick wave and indicated that he'd grab himself some lunch, then join her.

He'd been a bit reluctant when she'd suggested it. Even though they'd only told Roxy about their unconventional set-up, he understood that they would become the focus of gossip. Which he didn't like.

Plus, every time he was in Natalie's company he found himself fighting his needs. Soaking her in. Admiring the colour of her eyes. That little side-smile she sometimes did when something amused her. The wondrous way in which she laughed.

He loved working with her. She was very dedicated to her patients and he had no doubt that she would be a great mother. But...he couldn't let his feelings for her run away with him. He needed to keep up that wall. Because he'd been through a major loss before. He'd lost a child and a wife and he knew how devastating that could be. And what would be the point in getting attached to these babies and to Natalie if it happened again?

It was the only way he could keep his heart safe. Because he wasn't sure he could go through the trauma of losing those he loved again. Jenny, back in England, was still trying to rebuild her life, even after all this time. So best to try and not love at all.

But he felt that maybe he was already fighting a losing battle, because ever since she'd spilt that drink all over him in Liquid Nights on New Year's Eve, and looked up into his eyes with shock and apology, he'd been a little lost. She'd affected him from day one, and when he'd realised he was going to have to work with her he'd struggled.

Now she was carrying his twins. Precious, precious cargo! He couldn't believe he was being given another chance to become a father. All he wanted to do was wrap himself around her and keep her safe—because if he could do that, then maybe it would go some way towards atoning for what had happened to Jenny. Maybe it would show the world that he was worthy of having happiness. Having the family that he'd been craving for quite some time now.

He took his tray over to her table. Tea. A baked salmon fillet and a jacket potato. A small orange jelly with fruit pieces for dessert.

Henry sat opposite her, noted that she'd gone for the curry option, with some rice, and that she'd almost finished. 'Hey.'

'Hey, yourself.' She smiled.

'How are you feeling?' he asked.

'A bit better, I think. Nausea has eased up.'

'Maybe it's on its way out?'

'I hope so. It's been awful.'

He glanced over at a line of nurses standing in the queue, who all seemed to be stealing glances their way and whispering. 'Grapevine is in full swing. That didn't take long,' he said.

'Never does in a place like this. Is it bothering you?'

'Somewhat. I'm a very private person. Knowing that everyone here is aware of my private life is going to be a little difficult to deal with.'

'But you're not embarrassed?' she asked.

'About you? This? No.'

'Good.' She smiled. 'Because we need to be united for these babies. We have to be strong.'

He nodded.

'Speaking of which… I'm going to start looking for someplace else to live. I thought I'd better let you know. My place is a shoebox. Definitely not big enough for me and twins. And, yes, I know it's still early to be making plans, but it can take a long time to find a good place in the city.'

'I'll keep an eye out for you. Although…' He trailed off.

'Although what?'

He laughed. 'My apartment is big enough for us all.'

He shook his head, not quite believing what he might be offering.

Am I offering?

She stared at him. 'Are you suggesting I should move in? With you?'

He shrugged. He really didn't know. He'd thought about it, but not really come to any conclusions. He'd originally assumed the babies would live with Natalie and he would take them at weekends. But if her place was that tiny...

If he was going to get this miracle chance of being a father, he wanted to be there every minute of the day for them. He didn't want to be a part-time father!

'I want to be there for them as much as I can.'

'Which means what...for us?' She blushed.

'I don't know.'

'Are we going to be more involved than friends?' she asked quietly, clearly nervous, clearly ready to run if he said the wrong thing and embarrassed her.

She was talking about having a relationship with him. About them being a couple! And though he longed for it, he was scared of it, too. What if it all went wrong? Losing the babies would be bad enough...but losing Natalie, too?

Relationships could be precarious.

Every day you walked a very thin line.

'I don't know. I really don't,' he repeated.

'Do you not think of me in that way?'

He laughed. Was she being serious? He

thought about her in 'that way' all the time. That was the problem!

'I think of you in every way,' he answered, his voice quiet.

'That's good, isn't it?'

It was terrifying…that was what it was.

Because he hadn't directly answered her, she persisted with another question.

'What conclusion did you come to?'

He looked around them, checking that no one was close enough to overhear. 'Are you asking me to be in a relationship with you? A romantic relationship?'

Her cheeks flushed red and he realised he'd put her on the spot. But he needed to hear what she wanted. If he knew what she wanted, then maybe he could work out how *he* wanted to be involved in all of this.

'I don't know. Possibly. I only have one night to go off, but we seemed to get along very well. And I, for one, find myself thinking…sometimes…that we could…er…give it a go.'

'For the sake of the babies?' he said.

She looked at him strangely. 'What else?'

She'd certainly given him a lot to think about. She wanted a relationship with him! That had terrific appeal. He'd wondered about it, too. She was always in his mind, even when he was at home alone, ever since they'd met, and now she was telling him she wanted them to try to be together.

Was he brave enough?

Thankfully, he was saved by his mobile phone. An alert asking him to go back to OBGYN. He was being paged by Dr Yang.

'I've got to go.'

'Of course. But think about it, Henry. I don't want to screw this up.'

Nor did he. And perhaps that was the reason why he ought to stay away until the babies were safely here and he knew everything was all right?

It was clear to Natalie that Henry was only thinking of the babies. She'd asked him about the possibility of a relationship and that was what he'd replied. *For the sake of the babies?*

She felt upset, but acknowledged to herself that she had to be realistic. They had only spent one night together—they couldn't base an entire relationship on one night, a few lunch dates and an unexpected miracle pregnancy.

So she decided to focus on her work and entered the room of Jo and Richard Malbeck, who had come in to have their twins. Jo had naturally gone into labour at thirty-seven weeks and three days and was contracting regularly. Both babies were head-down, so that was good, too.

'These are your first babies?' she asked.

'Yes.'

'How exciting! I'm expecting twins, too,' she said, cradling her small rounded bump.

She was proud and yet also somehow shy about admitting it out loud to people. But she wanted to celebrate it. The pregnancy was going well right now, so why shouldn't she? She'd had enough bad stuff happen. It meant something for her to take the time to be happy when she could.

'Congratulations!' Jo said. 'It's scary, though, isn't it?'

Natalie laughed. 'Just a bit! Now, it says here in your birth plan that you want to stay as mobile as possible and try to have a water birth—is that right?'

'If I can.'

'I don't see why not. Everything's going smoothly right now. We'll monitor you closely, especially after the first baby is out, to make sure Baby B is in the right position for a head delivery. When the second twin suddenly gets that extra room after Baby A is out, it sometimes flips.'

'Dr Yang said that, too.'

'Feel free to move around. Take a walk… bounce on a ball. It all helps. You're five centimetres now, so I'll start filling the pool, and I'll let you know when you can get in, okay?'

'Thanks, Natalie.'

Jo got up from the bed now that she was off the monitoring trace and began to pace back and forth in the room.

Natalie wrote down in Jo's notes what she'd advised and her plan of action. She hoped that Jo would get to have the birth she'd dreamed of the same way Natalie had dreamed of her own future and her babies. But for Natalie her hopes went beyond the twins in her womb. She'd had aspirations for her and Henry, too, but could feel that hope dwindling. And it was tainting her dreams of having that perfect future she aspired to.

'I'll be back in a moment. The call bell is there, if you need me.'

Natalie headed back to the desk in the main corridor. She needed to order another warmer for the second baby and notify the NICU doctors that she had twins on the way—even though, for their gestation, they should be okay. It paid to be safe anyway.

She caught a glimpse of Henry at the end of the corridor. As usual, he looked absolutely gorgeous, completely unaware of the effect he had on her. She tried not to stare, to get on with her work, but found she couldn't tear her eyes away. And then he looked over too, and caught her eye.

For a moment they just looked at one another, and then Henry gave her a nod and headed into a patient's room.

She wished so badly that he would take a risk on them. But she understood his need to try and protect himself after his own past trauma.

I miss you.

'Hey, bro, what's up?'

Henry was all aflutter at Natalie's suggestion of having a relationship and he needed to talk to someone—so he'd called his brother.

'I need to ask your advice.'

'Sounds serious.'

'It is.'

'So, what's up?'

'You know that girl we were talking about? Who I met on New Year's Eve?'

'Yeah?'

'Well…' He sucked in a breath. 'She's pregnant. With my babies.'

'Babies? More than one?'

'Yep.'

'Wow.'

'I know. Tell me about it. I really, really like her, Hugh, and I think I've offered to let her come and stay with me when the babies arrive, because I don't want to miss being around them, but...'

'But you're scared?'

'Wouldn't you be?'

Even if Natalie wasn't pregnant, he'd be seriously doubting his rule not to get involved.

'There's definitely something between us. Something stronger than mere attraction. I consciously seek her out. I think about her *all the time*. She's never out of my mind. I feel better in her company. I feel lost when she's not there.'

'So, what's the problem, bro? That sounds great. Like you've got feelings...real feelings for her.'

'I have.'

'Then go for it. What'll happen if you don't? You could miss the chance to be really happy at last. I want that for you. After all you've been through.'

Henry nodded. Listened. It was just so hard to know what to do for the best and keep his heart safe.

Natalie alerted the front desk when Jo began to push. She was in the pool and doing well when Henry came in to assist with the delivery of her twins.

He glanced at Natalie and gave her a nod of acknowledgement. A quick smile.

She smiled back. 'She's been pushing for a couple of minutes.'

'Okay, let's see how you're doing, Jo.' He put on the longer gloves they used for pool deliveries, and dressed in a gown to cover his everyday clothes. 'Ah! I can already see a head of dark hair.'

'Definitely mine, then,' joked Richard, Jo's husband, who had a full head of dark hair himself.

'Not the time, honey...' breathed Jo.

Richard stroked her arm. 'You sure? I thought you always had time for my sparkling wit?'

Jo glared at him, then sucked in another breath before pushing again.

Natalie coached Jo through her breathing, counting from one to ten again and again, managing to get three counts per contraction so Jo could give her all. Beside her, Henry watched carefully, helping to facilitate the birth with careful manipulation of Jo's perineum and vulva to prevent tears.

'You're doing great, Jo. We might get the head out on the next one, so I'll need you to listen to me carefully, okay?'

Jo nodded, sucking in another breath and bearing down like a champ.

'Nearly there!' Richard encouraged, peering

down between his wife's legs, his face a mask of hope and excitement.

Jo growled with the effort, her face red, straining really hard.

"Little push for me…and another…okay, pant!' Henry instructed.

Natalie looked down. The head had crowned and was out, naturally turning towards Jo's right inner thigh, the little face was scrunched-up, the babyblissfully unaware of what awaited it in the world. As always, Natalie was in awe of the miracle of birth, and today it seemed even more miraculous, knowing that she might very well be doing this herself in just a few months!

Would Dr Yang deliver her babies? Would Roxy assist? Would Henry be mopping her brow and calling her *honey* and stroking her arm? Or would she be in a delivery room all alone?

The thought made her blood run cold and she looked at Henry, saw his face was a mask of concentration and determination. His strong arms were waiting, ready to catch this first baby.

He would be a good parent, she knew. And he wanted it as badly as she did. He must do, or she couldn't bear it.

'One more push, Jo!'

Jo bore down hard.

Henry smiled with delight as the first baby, a little girl, slid out into his waiting hands. He adjusted his grip and then lifted Jo and Richard's daughter up onto Jo's belly as Natalie draped the baby with a towel.

'Congratulations!'

Natalie caught Henry's eye then. He looked at her as if to say, *This could be us.*

At least that was how she interpreted it, anyway.

She smiled and nodded as Henry clamped the cord and Richard cut it. The baby burst into loud protest at her arrival, now that she was no longer in the lovely warmth of her mother's womb.

'I can't believe it! She's gorgeous!' Jo gasped.

'I'm so proud of you, honey.' Richard pressed his face to his wife's and kissed her on the cheek, before stooping to kiss his daughter.

Both Natalie and Henry smiled, enjoying this moment they got to share. Henry even winked at her!

Her stomach did a little flip. What did that wink mean?

It meant something, right? It meant something to her, anyway.

She knew Henry's reluctance to get into a relationship. Maybe this was his way of sending a silent message? *This could be us.* Something he couldn't say out loud in the room, because right now the moment was about Richard and Jo and *their* babies.

Whatever it was, she liked being included by him. Loved his secret smile, the twinkle in his eyes, the warm way he looked at her. It did incredible things to her insides!

'Honey, take the baby. Another contraction's starting.' Jo passed her newborn daughter over to her husband, who took the baby reverently, as if she was the most precious thing he'd ever had the privilege to hold.

Natalie wrapped another towel around the baby, saying, 'Keep her warm.' Then she returned to kneel by the pool again, as Jo began to breathe through her contraction.

'I need to check the position of the second baby, Jo—okay?' asked Henry.

'Okay…'

Henry performed the internal examination quickly, then withdrew. 'Good news. Baby's head down, so you can push with the next one.'

'I've already done this once. Do I really have to do it again?'

Henry smiled. 'I'm afraid so. There are no shortcuts with twins.'

He glanced at Natalie again.

He was right. There were no shortcuts. No

cheat codes. No magic button. Having twins was double the work, but double the reward.

Natalie tried to imagine herself holding one of their babies and Henry the other. The thought made her glow. Made her feel as if she wanted to pull Henry close and hold him tight.

Jo began to push again.

'You can do this!' urged Richard.

Natalie needed this birth to go well. She felt somehow that if it did then it would be a good sign for her own pregnancy. That their twins would get through this pregnancy safely, without any mishaps or dangers or emergency procedures.

'Just a couple of pushes to go,' she said, joining in with the encouragement.

It took four more pushes. Four hard, strenuous pushes. And then out popped a little baby boy. One of each!

Jo began to cry, as did her husband, and because of her hormones Natalie found she was fighting the strong urge to cry herself. She had to keep wiping at her eyes, and her face stretched wide into a smile as both babies were checked and found to be extremely healthy. No need to go to the NICU, APGARs were excellent, and the new little family were left alone to get used to each other.

* * *

Natalie headed to the linen room to get new sheets for the bed and Henry followed her in.

'That was amazing, wasn't it?' She turned to face him, her smile brighter than the sun.

'It was. It made me think of us.'

'Me too,' she answered, glad that he'd felt the magic of that moment as well.

For a moment they just stood there, looking at one another. Natalie felt a yearning inside her that was so strong she wasn't sure she'd be able to contain it. The need to touch him. Just once. To feel him in her arms again. Her hunger for him burned like a flare, white-hot, and she could see in his eyes that he wanted her, too.

But then an alarm bell sounded and they were ripped violently from the moment, knowing they had to push aside whatever it was that they themselves wanted and answer the call.

Henry led the charge, bursting from the linen room, his eyes scanning the corridor to see the red alarm light strobing wildly outside Room Eleven.

They both ran as fast as they could, bursting into the room to see a woman on the bed, writhing in pain, her baby's head already out, and Roxy looking up at them in a panic.

'This is Clare. A late walk-in. Baby's head

was out when she got here and now it's a shoulder dystocia.'

Natalie rushed to Clare's side as Henry donned gloves and immediately began to assess the situation.

'Page Dr Yang,' he ordered, as other staff ran into the room. 'How long has she been pushing?' he asked Roxy.

'She can't remember.'

Natalie could feel her heart in her throat. A shoulder dystocia was one of the most terrifying things to happen in a birthing suite. A true emergency. Staff would have only minutes to get the baby out safely.

Clare writhed on the bed. 'Help me!'

Natalie's heart ached.

'Don't push yet,' Henry said. 'We need to release baby's shoulder from behind your pubic bone first.'

A nurse rushed back into the room. 'Dr Yang is in the OR, Dr Locke.'

Henry nodded, and Natalie knew he would be feeling the pressure of being the only doctor there at the moment, having to make decisions and deliver this baby to its mother, keeping them both safe.

In that instant she admired his fortitude and bravery. He did not shirk from his duty, he did not dither, and he knew what he had to do.

'Let's get her into the McRoberts Manoeuvre.'

McRoberts involved getting the patient to lie on her back with her legs pushed outwards and upwards, towards her chest.

'I'm going to press firmly here—okay?' Henry told Clare, positioning his hand on her abdomen, just above her pubic bone, trying to manipulate the baby from above.

But Natalie could see that, although it had helped somewhat, there still wasn't enough room for the baby. 'What about an episiotomy?' she suggested.

'I agree. Clare, I'm going to have to make a cut to help ease the baby out—okay?'

'Do whatever you need to! Just get it out!'

It was over in a matter of seconds. As soon as Henry made the cut, then applied abdominal pressure again, the shoulder was released and the baby slithered out, its face screwing up into an almighty roar on arrival.

A palpable relief filled the room. Natalie looked across to Roxy, who grinned, and then she looked at Henry, who gave her a quick smile before returning to his work.

'Is it okay?' asked Clare, who couldn't see her baby as it was surrounded by staff over at the warmer.

'Baby's doing great,' said one of the paediatricians. 'We'll have him over to you in just a moment.'

Clare sank back against the pillows. 'Thank God! And thank you, guys. Thank you so much!'

'Hey, you did all the work,' Henry said, busy stitching.

'But you saved us.'

'All in a day's work.'

The baby was brought over to Clare moments later, with the paediatrician explaining that sometimes babies born after a shoulder dystocia suffered from something called a brachial plexus injury—a stretching of the brachial nerve. But any numbness or discomfort should pass after a few days.

Clare herself had suffered some tears, as well as the episiotomy, but her bleeding was well controlled and she'd only need a few extra days of rest.

They all left Mom and baby to bond, and Natalie got ready to head for home. It had been a long day.

'Setting off?'

Henry stood in the doorway to the staff room, leaning against the doorjamb, arms folded, stethoscope still draped around his neck. He looked so yummy in that moment that Natalie had to turn away and take her time getting her stuff from her locker.

'Yes. I'm ready for a hot bath.'

'Not too hot, I hope?'

She smiled, closing her locker. 'No, don't worry.'

She walked over to stand before him, her coat draped over one arm.

'What you did in that room was amazing.'

'It's what I'm trained for.'

'But you saved that baby's life.'

'We all did.'

She smiled. 'Don't be so modest. You're an amazing man, Henry Locke, and I know, in my heart, that you're going to make an amazing father, too.'

He looked at her then, in such a way that caused everything else in the world to just fall away. Sounds muted...details blurred. All she could see was his eyes and the need in them. The yearning. The want. Her whole body was responding in kind, and before she knew what was happening Henry had moved towards her in a rush, taking her face in his hands and bringing her lips to his in a sweet, gentle kiss, as if fearing that if he waited he would change his mind.

Natalie dropped her coat as she brought her hands up to hold him tightly against her, moaning slightly as his kiss deepened and her every nerve-ending sprang into action, awaiting a caress, a touch...

Being kissed by Henry was even more magical now than it had been on New Year's Eve! Maybe it was the fact that she'd had to wait so long to enjoy it again, or maybe it was because this time they knew each other, so it was different and held more meaning.

No longer were they strangers who'd met on a night out—two lonely souls, each with a heartbreak they'd been trying to hide. Now they knew each other's pain. Now they were stepping forward into something new. She was carrying his children. Her hormones were raging. And the intensity of Henry's kiss was mind-blowing. Earth-shattering.

She needed more. Wanted more. But suddenly he took hold of her upper arms and pushed himself away from her, letting go and taking a step back.

'I'm sorry. I...' He met her gaze then, and she saw in his eyes a deep grief, before he turned and walked away.

'Henry!' she called after him, her heart breaking.

What had just happened?

The kiss had been amazing. How could he regret that?

'Henry Locke! Don't make me run after you!' she called.

Henry stopped. Turned. Came back to her. 'We can't do this. *I* can't do this.'

'Can't do what?'

'Allow myself to have feelings for you. It's too much. It's too difficult.'

He wasn't looking her in the eye.

'I'm sorry for kissing you just now. I should have stopped it before it even began. But I will be there for the babies, Natalie. Anything they need. *You* need. Moral support—whatever. But I can't do this…with you…right now. I'm sorry.'

And he walked away.

Tears were already trickling down her cheeks as he rounded the corner and disappeared from sight. It was as if he'd taken all her hopes and her dreams with her. Taken them from her. Given her hope, then stolen it away.

Just like Wade had.

He had made her think that everything was going to be okay. Let her dream. Let her make wishes for her future. And then he'd torn it all down, shown her that he wasn't available and that she was actually very much on her own.

How could Henry do this to her?

If they couldn't be together then…what was the point?

Would they be working together for ever-more and sharing their children? Would she be seeing him every day? Torturing herself with what might have been?

She'd never felt more alone than she had in that moment as he walked away.

At least Wade hadn't left her pregnant...

Suddenly Natalie didn't want to be there any more. Not in Heartlands. Not in New York. The yearning to run back home, back into the bosom of her family, was incredibly strong. She knew her parents missed her. Knew that they would rally round and be there for her as she raised these babies. And Montana was a lovely place to have kids. All that nature... Those wide-open spaces, the animals on the farm...

What did she have here? Her tiny apartment and traffic. No one to help her out.

I've made a terrible mistake. Again.

CHAPTER NINE

HENRY STOOD IN an empty patient's room, pacing back and forth, frustrated. Angry! Furious with himself! Why on earth had he *kissed* her? All it had done was prove to him how perfect they were for each other, how beautifully they fitted, how much he wanted more.

But the second—the very second—he'd realised he'd wanted every part of her, to be with her every day, to wake up with her, go to sleep with her, his brain had begun to scream at him.

This could all go wrong. You could lose these babies and her and then where will you be?

And he'd panicked. Plain and simple. He'd not thought it through. He'd allowed his desires to overrun his brain. Had given in to his need for her and tasted her lips one last time. Fireworks had gone off inside his brain. His entire body had lit up with energy. His desire had been soaring into the atmosphere as he'd tried to soak up every last drop of her. And it had been that need, that yearning, that had warned him…

What if you lose this…? Think of what it will do to you…

He'd had to stop. Before he got in too deep. Before he fell in love. Or perhaps it was already too late for that? But something terrible might happen, and to have his heart ripped out from his chest once again wasn't to be borne.

The pregnancy might not last—and even if it did, what if the same thing happened afterwards? What if Natalie got postnatal depression? What if she suffered psychosis, the same way Jenny had? What if? What if? *What if?*

There was too much that was unknown. Too much he had no control over whatsoever. And he couldn't deal with that. That was the whole point about not getting involved with someone! You never knew how they were going to be. Okay, so Jenny had bipolar. She'd shown signs that her mental health wasn't great even before the pregnancy—and, yes, she'd stopped taking the tablets that kept her stable whilst she was pregnant.

But that had had nothing to do with their baby being stillborn. And lightning could strike twice.

The dread he'd felt ever since finding out about the twins had to count for something, didn't it? If you didn't listen to your own logic, then what was the point? He *could* be with Natalie—just not yet. He had to wait until he knew for sure that they were all safe. And then, and only then, could he possibly allow himself to venture down the road of allowing himself to become involved.

Just not now. Not whilst they were all still in danger. To do anything otherwise would be crazy, and risky—not only to his heart, but to his sanity.

I've made the right decision.

Only why did he feel so awful about it?

It was just a short break. That was all she would tell herself. A short break back home. Some time away to think. To get her head straight. Talk to her mom and dad. See what they thought. And if they all agreed she should stay in Montana, then that was what she would do. She'd send in her resignation, effective immediately, to Heartlands Hospital, and leave New York and Henry Locke behind her.

This was such a difficult time in her life. Being let go by Henry. Cast adrift in a sea of abandonment. That was what it felt like. Maybe she was too sensitive after what Wade had done to her, but it was how she felt. The desire to be surrounded by family, by people she *knew* loved her, was strong.

But if she left then she'd be walking away from the medical care that Dr Yang, a specialist in problem multiple pregnancies, could provide—and surely, her babies' wellbeing, not hers, should come first?

Look at me...casting aspersions on Henry for doing that when I know I need to do so myself.

Wasn't Henry just being sensible? Hers was a high-risk pregnancy. Twins. Prior uterine surgery. Internal scarring. Previous broken pelvis. And then there was the fact that Jenny's baby had been stillborn. They'd had no idea why. Was it something that had just happened? Or was there a reason for it in Henry's DNA?

She felt like a ticking human time bomb.

Was Henry so wrong to insist on there being some sort of distance between them? He was just protecting himself—and why wouldn't he, after all that he'd been through? Hadn't both of them been trying to protect themselves by vowing to remain single when they'd first met?

But deep down Natalie had hoped that Henry would care for her so much that he wouldn't be able to bear being apart from her. And the fact that he clearly didn't...that he'd so easily pushed her away...

That hurt.

Natalie stared down at her suitcase. She'd packed it earlier, crying all the while, shoving things in without properly folding them, grabbing stuff without really thinking about what to take.

Am I being hasty?

The buzzer on her door sounded. 'Taxi,' said a man's voice.

Natalie bit her lip and grabbed her suitcase off the bed.

The next day, Henry made it into the hospital feeling awful. He hadn't slept a wink. He hadn't been able to do anything but think of how it had felt to kiss Natalie yesterday. How it had felt to have her in his arms once again and how awful he had made himself feel by ending the kiss and pushing himself away from her.

The look in her eyes when he had done so...

Betrayal. Upset. Shock.

Disbelief.

She wanted more for them—he knew that. And so did he. But if he allowed himself to fully admit what he felt for her, the way he knew he should, then he would be putting himself at risk. And if something awful were to happen to these babies, or to Natalie, then she would need someone who could be strong for her. And how strong could he be if he was crumbling inside? He wasn't good enough for her right now. Not strong enough.

He was doing them both a favour, really.

He saw Roxy first, when he walked onto the floor. She was at the desk, just hanging up the phone, a pen shoved through the rough bun of her brunette hair.

'What did you do?' she asked curtly, one eyebrow raised.

He frowned. 'I'm sorry?'

'Natalie. She's taken some leave. But she called me last night, almost in tears, saying she needed some time to think, and when a girlfriend says that kind of thing to me, in that way, I know a boy's involved. So come on—what did you do?'

The look of hurt in Natalie's eyes flashed into his mind once again. 'How long has she taken leave for?'

Roxy shrugged. 'Don't know. But she was talking about going back home.'

'To her apartment?'

'To Montana, you fool! I mean...um...' she blushed '... Dr Locke.'

Henry stared at her in shock. Natalie was on leave? Might already have left New York? The idea that she might be gone… Out of reach! He didn't even know exactly where her home was. He might never see her again! Might never see his babies. And if she had to go through this all alone…he'd never forgive himself.

He'd never intended that to happen. He'd sworn to Natalie that he would be there for her in some way. But if she'd gone into some sort of hiding, what could he do?

'When did she say she was leaving?'

'I don't know.'

He rushed past Roxy.

'Where are you going?' she yelled. 'There's no one to cover the floor if an emergency comes in!'

Henry skidded to a stop. He needed to get to Natalie! But he couldn't put anyone else at risk.

'Where's Dr Yang?'

'Not here yet.'

'What about Dr Chatwin?'

'In the OR.'

He sighed. 'Okay. I'll wait until she's back on the floor—then I'm going.'

'To do what?'

'Beg Natalie to stay.'

Henry burst from the lift, looking left and right at the apartment numbers, then sprinted down to Natalie's door at the far end of the corridor. His fist hammered the door.

'Natalie! *Natalie!*'

He waited briefly, but impatience overrode him.

'Natalie? Please answer the door. I don't know if you can hear me, or if you're even in there, but if you are, please let me in!'

'Who are you?'

A door behind him opened and a stout woman with flushed cheeks looked out at him curiously.

'Is Natalie in, do you know?'

The woman shrugged. 'I don't know. But could you be a little more quiet, please?'

He nodded. 'Sorry.'

The woman stared at him a moment more, then closed her door.

Henry rested his head against Natalie's front door.

'You're probably gone already. I bet that I'm too late. But...' He sighed. 'I just wanted to say I'm sorry. Sorry for pushing you away. I got... scared. You mean so much to me and... I just kept thinking that things could all still go so wrong, and I wouldn't be strong enough to help you. I thought that if I kept my distance then somehow it would be easier. But then I heard from Roxy that you were taking time off to go home, and the idea that I'd never see you again just made me realise that…'

He closed his eyes in pain, trying not to accept that this might have already happened.

But then there was a click from the other side of the door, and he took a startled step back as Natalie opened it, red-eyed from crying.

'You're still here?'

She nodded, crossing her arms. 'I am.'

'You heard everything I just said?'

'I did.'

'I meant every word. The idea that you might be gone for ever was…just awful. It made me realise that even if something bad did happen to you, or to the babies, then I'd still want to be there for you. That I couldn't bear the thought that you'd be alone. Or that I would.'

'What are you saying?'

'I'm saying that I want to be with you and that… I think I love you.'

Natalie flushed and gave a small smile. 'You only think?'

He shook his head. 'I know that I do. And I know that I need you in my life every single day. With me.'

'So tell me properly.'

He smiled.

'Natalie Webber. You and I have already been through so much. The last few months have been crazy for both of us, and I want to continue experiencing the crazy with you. I want to be there with you through hard times and good times, and I want to be able to touch you and hold you in my arms and keep you safe. You're my first thought every day. I think of you constantly. I miss you when you're not with me. I rush to be with you. Seek you out. And not in a weird, stalker way.'

He smiled again.

'I want to stare into your eyes for ever and never let go.' He reached for her fingertips and locked them in his own. 'I love you.'

She smiled. 'I love you, too.'

'So this means…?'

'That we're both in a bit of a pickle!'

'But we're in it together?' he asked.

Natalie nodded and stepped closer still. 'I was going to leave. But then I thought of all the medical help the twins might need and I knew I had to put them first. And that's when I realised that that was what you'd been doing, too. Only I blamed you for acting that way, when really it was exactly what you should have been doing. I wanted you to love me, but I didn't think that you would. That you *could*.'

'Loving you is easy enough. Admitting it was slightly harder.'

'We might have some tough times ahead of us, Henry.'

'We might.' He tucked a stray curl behind her ear. 'But I think we can get through anything if we're together.'

'I think so, too.'

And then he kissed her.

And this time the kiss was even more euphoric than the last. Because this time they knew that they were destined to be together and that neither of them was hiding from the other at all. They'd both admitted their love, both admitted their fears and their flaws, and it was still all okay.

Love was what mattered in the end.

EPILOGUE

HENRY UNLOCKED THE DOOR, pushing it open wide, allowing Natalie to walk through first. His apartment had changed in the last few months. Gone was all the dark furniture, glass and chrome, and the place had had new life breathed into it by her own home decorating. There was a cream couch with scatter cushions. A fluffy rug. A low coffee table strewn with books, and a glass bowl filled with fresh cut flowers. The walls had bookcase after bookcase, and now there were photos of the two of them all around the room.

They walked into the living space and put down the two car seats, side by side, then stepped back to look down at their twin baby girls: Sophie and Esme.

'So what do we do now?' Natalie asked, and she slid her arm around his waist as she stared down at the babies.

'I don't know. I've never got this far.'

'There's not a handbook?'

He laughed. 'I'm afraid not.'

They both just stared at the two girls, falling in love with them even more. They looked so perfect.

Sophie had been born first, emerging into the world at just over thirty-three weeks with a strong cry, and weighing five pounds exactly. Esme—smaller, quieter, and more content at just four pounds twelve—had come into the world with a little snuffle, content to just be held.

Even though they weren't identical, they looked as if they could be. But in the last few weeks in the hospital they had begun to notice the tiny differences between the two girls. Esme had more hair and Sophie had her father's eyes.

'Why don't you sit down?' said Henry. 'I'll make us both a cup of tea. The girls will be awake soon and want feeding.'

Natalie nodded, sinking into the soft couch, glad to be back at home, surrounded by her own furnishings. She kicked off her boots and just sat there, staring at her two daughters. They were so perfect! So beautiful!

Eventually Henry came back through from the kitchen with a tray. There was a white teapot and two cups in saucers, a small plate of biscuits, and a dark blue velvet box.

Natalie frowned and looked up at him. 'What's that?'

Henry sank to the couch beside her and took the box, smiling. He opened it, then turned it around for Natalie to see.

Inside was a beautiful platinum ring, set with a large square cut diamond.

'I love you with all my heart and you have made me the happiest man in the world. Not just because you've given me two beautiful darling daughters, who I hope grow up to be exactly like their mother, but also because you've given me your heart and your soul, and I can't imagine my life without you in it. So, Natalie… Will you do me the honour of becoming my wife?'

Henry slipped off the couch and sank to one knee.

Natalie gasped, her hands clasped over her mouth in shock. 'Yes! I will!'

She threw her arms around him and pulled him tight, kissing his face, his cheeks, his mouth, feeling tears of happiness well up in her eyes as she held out her hand for him to slip the ring on.

She stared at it as it caught the light. A perfect fit.

Henry kissed her again, more passionately this time, but Sophie and Esme chose that moment to begin to snuffle awake.

Natalie held Henry's face in her hands, staring deeply into his eyes. 'I love you so much.'

'I love you more.'

The twins began to protest, wriggling in their respective car seats, wanting to get out.

Natalie laughed, wiping away her tears. 'Take one each?' she asked.

Henry nodded. 'Let's do this!'

* * * * *

If you enjoyed this story, check out these other great reads from Louisa Heaton

A Date with Her Best Friend
Their Marriage Worth Fighting For
Their Marriage Meant To Be
A GP Worth Staying For

All available now!